Red Berries
White Clouds
Blue Sky

Red Berries
White Clouds
Blue Sky

NEW YORK TIMES BESTSELLING AUTHOR

SANDRA DALLAS

PUBLISHED BY SLEEPING BEAR PRESS

Copyright © 2014 Sandra Dallas

Library of Congress Cataloging-in-Publication Data

Dallas, Sandra.
Red berries, white clouds, blue sky / written by Sandra Dallas.
pages cm
Summary: "After Pearl Harbor is bombed by the Japanese, twelve-year-old Tomi and her Japanese-American family are split up and forced to leave their California home to live in internment camps in New Mexico and Colorado" — Provided by the publisher.
ISBN 978-1-58536-906-5 (hard cover) — ISBN 978-1-58536-907-2 (paperback)
1. Japanese Americans—Evacuation and relocation, 1942-1945—Juvenile fiction. [1. Japanese Americans—Evacuation and relocation, 1942-1945—Fiction. 2. World War, 1939-1945—United States—Fiction.] I. Title.
PZ7.D1644Re 2014
[Fic]—dc23
2014004561

ISBN 978-1-58536-906-5 (case)
ISBN 978-1-58536-907-2 (paper)

1 2 3 4 5 6 7 8 9 10

Cover illustration by Mick Wiggins

Printed in the United States.

Sleeping Bear Press™

315 E. Eisenhower Parkway, Suite 200
Ann Arbor, Michigan 48108

© 2014 Sleeping Bear Press
visit us at sleepingbearpress.com

For Forrest and his cousins — Bodi, Alex, and Nicholas

TABLE *of* CONTENTS

1944

1945

1942 | CHAPTER ONE
THE SIGN *on the* DOOR

TOMI stopped just outside the grocery store where her mother always shopped and peered through the glass in the door's window. She loved the smells inside, of sawdust on the floor and of the bread that came in bright wrappers. Just beyond the door, she knew, were orderly displays of fresh fruit and vegetables—fat strawberries in green baskets, rows of corn covered by papery husks, cabbages as big as a baby's head.

Most of all, Tomi loved the candy displayed in the big glass case. With a penny in her hand, she would choose from among the jumble of Tootsie Rolls, inky black licorice, and other sweets. Today, she thought, looking through the glass, she would pick two jawbreakers from a glass bowl. The jawbreakers were two for a penny, which meant she and her brother Hiro could each have one.

She pushed the door open and heard the jingle of the bell that announced customers entering the store. But just before she stepped onto the old wooden floor, she spotted a sign taped to the window. Her mouth dropped open, and she stopped so abruptly that Hiro ran into her.

"What's wrong?" he asked.

Tomi turned around. "I left the penny at school," she said.

"It's in your hand," he told her.

Tomi looked down at her fingers, which clutched the coin. "We're not going in there."

"Why not?" Hiro asked.

Tomi took her brother's hand and tried to pull him away, but Hiro refused to move. Then he spied the sign on the door. "What's that sign say?" he asked.

"I can't read it," Tomi said quickly.

"You're twelve, and you can so read it. I'm seven, and I can read, too." He squinted as he sounded out the words. Then he looked up at his sister. "It says 'No Japs.' That's not a very nice word, is it?"

Tomi shook her head and tugged at her brother.

"Mom says the word is 'Japanese.' 'Jap' is a mean word,"

Hiro said. He read the sign again, then grinned. "It's okay, Tomi. We're not Japanese. We're Americans. We can go in."

Just then, a man in a white apron came to the door and stared at Tomi and Hiro.

"Hi, Mr. Akron," Hiro said. He and Tomi had bought candy from Mr. Akron ever since they could remember.

Mr. Akron looked uncomfortable. He made a shooing motion with his hand. "Go on, kids. Scram. Can't you read the sign?" He wiped his hands on his apron.

Tomi stared at him a moment, then said, "Come on, Hiro. Let's go. They don't want us here. Besides, who cares about that old candy anyway?" She looked at the ground instead of at her brother or the grocer. Her face was red as she stared at the sidewalk, wishing her mother had never given her the penny. She wanted to be anywhere but in front of the store where the man thought she was a *Jap*.

"How come we can't come in?" Hiro asked.

The grocer ran his finger around the inside of his collar. "You Japs bombed Pearl Harbor," he said, then turned and went inside, closing the door.

"Me and Tomi didn't bomb anybody," Hiro called through the glass, but Mr. Akron ignored him.

"Come *on*, Hiro!" Tomi yanked her brother along the

sidewalk. She walked with her head down. Her hair hid her face; she hoped nobody would recognize her. She had never been so embarrassed in her life.

"I don't understand. What's Pearl Harbor?" Hiro asked, stumbling along beside his sister. "Why won't he sell us candy?"

Tomi turned the corner and headed toward a park. It was the long way home, but they weren't likely to run into any kids they knew, and that was good. She didn't want anyone to find out what had just happened.

They reached a bench, and Tomi sat down, Hiro next to her.

"What's Pearl Harbor?" Hiro asked again.

Tomi took a deep breath. "It's a place in Hawaii. The Japanese bombed our American ships there, and lots of sailors were killed."

"Jeepers!" Hiro tried to whistle through his teeth, but his front teeth were missing, so the sound came out like a rush of wind. "How come they did that?"

Tomi shook her head. "I don't know. I heard it on the radio, and I heard Mom and Pop talk about it, but they stopped when they found out I was listening. So I don't understand everything. I just know President Roosevelt declared war on Japan."

"But why won't Mr. Akron let us into his store?"

"I guess he thinks we're spies or something, you know, like they talk about on the radio."

Hiro thought that over, then asked, "Spies? Who are we supposed to spy for?"

"Japan," Tomi answered.

"But we've never been there. Heck, Tomi, we don't even speak Japanese."

"Mom and Pop both came from Japan, and our grandparents *Jiji* and *Baba* still live there."

"We don't even know them," Hiro said.

Tomi shrugged. "I don't understand it, either. We say the Pledge of Allegiance every day in school, and we salute the flag. Pop always told us he and Mom were the best Americans because they *chose* to live in this country; they *chose* for you and me and Roy to be born here." Roy, their older brother, was almost sixteen.

"Are we going to tell Mom about the sign?" Hiro asked.

Tomi looked down at Hiro. "I don't know. Maybe we should so that she doesn't shop there." Tomi didn't like the idea that Mr. Akron might be rude to her mother.

The two of them sat on the bench, not talking for a

few minutes. It was winter, and although snow didn't fall in their southern California town not far from the ocean, the weather was cold. Tomi felt the chill and shivered. She started to tuck her hands into the sleeves of her sweater, then realized she was still holding the penny. "Those jaw-breakers would probably break our teeth. I don't want one anyway," she told her brother.

"Me neither," Hiro said. He grinned, and Tomi punched his arm.

"Besides, you don't have enough teeth to chew one," she said.

1942 | CHAPTER TWO

POP *and the* FBI

TOMI loved their little farmhouse. It was painted yellow, the color of the sun, Tomi's favorite color. An American flag hung from a pole in the yard. Pop raised it every day, while Tomi, Hiro, and Roy stood beside him. Then he lowered it at night, choosing one of the children to help him fold it. The flag was kept in a carved box next to the front door. Tomi was proud when she saw the red, white, and blue flag flying from its pole in front of the house.

Pop grew strawberries that were even bigger and redder than the ones in Mr. Akron's store. Pop didn't own the farm. He had come to America from Japan when he was younger. He told his children since he was born in Japan, he was an *Issei*, or first-generation American. The law said *Issei* couldn't own land in America. Pop's real name was Osamu, but everybody called him Sam. Mom, whose name was Sumiko, was an *Issei*, too. Tomi and her brothers, Hiro and Roy, were born in America. Pop explained that they were *Nisei*, or second-generation Americans.

It didn't matter that Pop just rented the farm, however. He had worked it since before Tomi was born, and the farm was the only home she'd ever known. Pop rented the land from Mr. Lawrence, who lived a mile away in a big house with white pillars in front. His daughter, Martha, was Tomi's best friend. They played together all the time in Martha's big house or in Tomi's tiny yellow cottage.

Mr. Lawrence's brand new Ford motor car was parked in front of the Itano house along with a car Tomi didn't recognize. Mr. Lawrence believed in Ford cars and bought one every two years. He'd encouraged Pop to buy a used Ford truck the year before. Pop had never owned a truck, and he was proud of it. He and Roy washed it every Saturday.

Mr. Lawrence stood on the porch with a man in a suit and hat. The two of them were hidden behind a trumpet vine and didn't see Tomi and Hiro as they came down the road.

"Sam Itano's as good an American as I am," Tomi heard

Mr. Lawrence say. His voice was loud and angry.

"Then why did he buy so much fertilizer? And gasoline, too? I'm betting it's for the Japanese submarines. They've been spotted off the coast." The second man didn't look much older than Roy.

"Look around you. This is a farm. You need gasoline to run the equipment. Sam's a smart farmer. He's stocking up on gas before it gets scarce. Besides, submarines don't run on gasoline," Mr. Lawrence told him.

"That's beside the point," the man wearing the suit said.

"Then what is the point?" Mr. Lawrence asked.

"Sam Itano's a Jap."

"Around here, we call him a Japanese," Mr. Lawrence said.

A third man came out of the house. He had Pop's newspaper in his hand and held it high so the others could see. "Look at this. It's in Japanese."

"That's Sam's newspaper. Are you saying it's illegal to read a newspaper written in another language?" Mr. Lawrence asked.

"It is if it's subversive."

"What's subversive?" Hiro asked. His voice carried.

Tomi whispered, "I think it means 'doing something against the government.' "

The men on the porch hadn't noticed the two children until now. One asked if they were the Itano kids. When Tomi nodded, he asked, "Your dad have a radio?"

Tomi didn't like the way the man sounded. *Is there something wrong with having a radio?* she wondered. She was about to tell them she didn't know. But Hiro belted out, "You bet! It's a Philco, brand-new. We got it for Christmas. It's swell."

The two men looked at each other. "And he listens to it, does he? What does he listen to?"

"Oh, everything," Hiro said, before Tomi could stop him. "He listens to *Blondie* and *Fibber McGee and Molly*. And when he's not home, Mom listens to *Backstage Wife* and *Our Gal Sunday*. Pop says they're dumb."

"They're soap operas," Tomi explained.

"I bet he listens to Japanese programs, too, doesn't he?" one of the men asked.

"There aren't any Japanese programs on the radio," Tomi told him.

The two men looked at each other, while Mr. Lawrence muttered, "Ha!"

Pop came out of the house then and motioned for Tomi and Hiro to go to him. Tomi wondered where Mom was; probably working in the strawberry fields. Pop was sweating, and he had a worried look on his face. He jingled the coins in his pocket. He did that when he was nervous. The day Pop arrived in America, he found a silver dollar on the street. It was his lucky coin, and he always carried it. Now he thumped the small coins in his pocket against the big silver dollar.

Tomi asked Pop about the two men, and he whispered, "They're from the FBI."

"Wow! The FBI, like in the movies!" Hiro said. "Are you going to help them capture some bad guys, Pop?"

Tomi knew the FBI agents weren't there to ask for Pop's help.

One of the men asked Tomi, "Does your father use the radio late at night?"

"Sure, he listens to *One Man's Family*," Tomi said.

The agent looked annoyed. "Does he use it to talk to the Japs?"

"Japanese." Mr. Lawrence reminded him.

Hiro laughed. "Boy, is he dumb. You don't talk to a radio," he whispered.

"Keep still, boy," the agent who'd come out of the house said. He turned to the other man. "You should see what he's got in there—Japanese books, letters, even a picture of the Emperor. We better take him in."

Mr. Lawrence stepped between Pop and the men. "On what grounds?" he asked.

"Espionage," the FBI man said.

"That's spying," Tomi told Hiro before he could ask.

Pop glanced from the two agents to Mr. Lawrence. "How can that be? I'm an American."

"You're not a citizen, are you?"

"I can't be. The law doesn't let *Issei* become citizens," Pop explained.

"You had a camera. What were you taking pictures of?" The agent was holding Pop's camera in his hand, the back of it open.

"My strawberry plants. And my children. You'd see if you hadn't exposed the film."

"Oh yeah?" The man took out a pair of handcuffs and motioned for Pop to put his wrists together in front of his waist. As the men led him to their car, Pop wouldn't look back at Tomi and Hiro. It was hard for Tomi to look at him, too.

"You kids tell your mother I'll be back later to explain what's going on," Mr. Lawrence said. Then he turned to Pop. "Don't worry, Sam. This isn't right. I'll get a lawyer for you. He'll prove you're a good American and shouldn't be arrested."

"Don't bother," one of the FBI men said. "It won't do him any good." Then he turned to Tomi and Hiro and said, "You kids, you tell your mother you're not to go more than five miles from here. And there's a curfew. That means you're not to be out after dark."

★

Mom had been working with the strawberry plants and hadn't known what had just happened. After all, people were always stopping by to buy strawberries. Pop always talked to them, because Mom was shy around strangers. As soon as Mr. Lawrence drove off, Tomi and Hiro ran to her, careful not to step on the strawberry plants.

"The FBI took Pop away. They put handcuffs on him," Hiro called to her.

"What?" Mom had been stooped over the plants, and she looked up, then rose slowly.

"They called him un-American," Tomi said. "I'm scared, but Mr. Lawrence said not to worry, that he'd get a lawyer to help Pop."

Mom put her hands over her face and stood that way for a long time. "I told him to get rid of those letters, those newspapers," she said to herself. She took her children's hands, and they walked back to the house.

When they went inside, Mom gasped at the mess the FBI agents had left. She always kept the house tidy. But now, drawers were pulled out in the bedroom and clothes dumped onto the floor. Dishes and canned goods had been taken from kitchen shelves and set on the table. The back of the radio had been pried off. Pop's letters from *Jiji* and *Baba* in Japan were scattered about. "Oh," Mom said, and sat down in a chair.

Tomi offered to put things away, but her mother said no. "We'll burn all this. I told your father to do that, but he said that everything would be all right."

Tomi and Hiro gathered up the papers that had been thrown onto the floor and put them into the stove. Mom picked up the picture of the Japanese emperor and placed it on top of the papers. Then she went into her bedroom and took down a wall scroll with a picture of a Japanese mountain on it and added it. Finally, she went to the closet for her best kimono. It was a beautiful turquoise silk dress she wore on special occasions. She shoved it into the stove. She cried when she lit a match and watched the silk catch fire. "We have to get rid of everything Japanese so that we can show we aren't aiding the enemy," she said.

"What about my doll?" Tomi asked. Her grandparents had sent her a Japanese doll with long black hair and bangs just like Tomi's. Her name was Janice. Tomi was too old to play with dolls, but she loved Janice too much to give her up.

Mom shook her head. "Surely, they can't object to a doll."

Tomi and Hiro sat beside their mother and watched as the fire burned. "I don't understand," Hiro said at last. "What did Pop do?"

"Nothing," Mom replied. "He didn't do anything. It's because he's Japanese."

"No he's not. He's an American," Hiro insisted.

Mom nodded, and then she asked Tomi to fix tea.

Tomi filled the kettle with water and placed it on the stove. She let the water boil, then set it aside a minute to cool before she poured it over the tea leaves in the teapot. The finest tea, Tomi knew, required hot, not boiling, water. After letting the tea steep, she poured it into blue-and-white china cups, each with a different design. Tomi picked up her mother's cup and handed it to her, wondering if they would have to get rid of the tea set.

Mom carried the tea to the table, and Tomi and Hiro sat down on either side of her. Hiro gulped his drink, but Tomi held her cup in her hand, letting the warmth rise and fill her nose with the sweet smell of tea.

"As you know, your father came to America from Japan when he was eighteen years old," Mom began. Tomi and Hiro had heard that story many times, but Mom always started at the beginning, and so she repeated how Pop had come to the United States because he thought there were more opportunities here for a boy like him. Pop got a job on a farm, laboring long hours at back-breaking work. He believed that was the way to get ahead. He saved his money and rented a few acres of farmland, where he grew strawberries.

The farm was successful. So he sent to Japan for a "picture bride." Picture brides were Japanese girls who wanted to marry Japanese men living in America. They sent their photographs to what was called a marriage broker. Pop chose Sumiko. She wasn't the prettiest of the girls whose pictures he studied, but she looked like the sweetest. Sam thought she would be a worker, too. So he paid her way to America, and they were married.

They were a good match. Sam and Sumiko cared about each other just as much as any American couple who had married for love. Many times, Tomi had seen her father take the picture bride photograph out of his wallet and smile at it.

"Your pop wanted us all to be Americans. That's why we speak English at home and wear American clothes. America's made up of people from all over the world," Mom said. She reminded Tomi and Hiro that the immigrants were Americans now, but they hadn't forgotten their foreign cultures. That was why the Mexicans in California ate tortillas and chili and sang beautiful songs in Spanish and the Germans held a harvest festival where they served beer and bratwurst. The Japanese weren't any different. Mom fixed spaghetti and tuna fish casseroles along with Japanese food and dressed just like other women in California, wearing a kimono only on special occasions.

Tomi knew all that, and she squiggled in her chair,

wishing her mother would get on with it.

Finally, Mom did. "Everything was all right until Japanese planes bombed Pearl Harbor last December and America declared war on Japan. Some Caucasians— white people—think we're spies just because we came from Japan. They believe we'll help the Japanese invade America."

"Invade means 'land here,'" Tomi explained to Hiro.

"I already know that," he said.

"These people think we're loyal to Japan instead of America," Mom continued.

"But can't they see our flag?" Hiro asked. "And don't they know we say the Pledge of Allegiance and Pop decorated his truck with red, white, and blue crepe paper for the Fourth of July parade?"

Mom looked down. "They say it doesn't matter, that we're only trying to trick them into believing we're loyal."

"Why would they take Pop?" Hiro asked.

Mom shook her head. "This is war. People are scared."

"They're scared of *us*?" Tomi looked at her brother, then at her mother, who wasn't much taller than Hiro. Tomi glanced at her reflection in the mirror across from the table. How could anyone be afraid of *her*?

"*Shikata ga nai*," Mom said. That was her favorite expression. Of course, it was a Japanese expression, but there was no reason it couldn't be used in America. It meant "It cannot be helped."

1942 | CHAPTER THREE
THE END *of* SCOUTING

R O Y burst through the door and threw his clarinet case onto a chair. Tomi's brother was in the school orchestra, and he and four other boys had their own band called the Jivin' Five. They played at school and church dances. "I ran into Mr. Lawrence down the road. He told me the FBI arrested Pop. What happened?"

"They think he's a spy," Hiro replied.

"They think we're all spies," Tomi added.

"For growing strawberries?"

"For being Japanese," Mom said.

Roy sat down and put his head in his hands. "I guess I shouldn't be surprised," he said. "Last week, a woman asked about hiring the Jivin' Five to play for a party, but she said she didn't want me there." The other members of the band were Caucasians.

"Jivin' Four doesn't sound like much," Tomi said.

"I guess we just have to wait until people figure out we're not the enemy."

★

But some people insisted the Itanos *were* the enemy.

A few days later, Tomi went to her friend Mary Jane Malkin's house for her weekly Girl Scout meeting. Tomi loved scouting. The members of her troop were her best friends. They had come to the Itano place in the fall to work on their merit badges for gardening. Pop had showed them how he planted the strawberries and cared for them. He'd let the scouts have a piece of land for their own garden. All the girls had gotten their gardening badges. Tomi had been the first. She worked hard to earn badges and had more than anyone else in her troop. And she'd sold more Girl Scout Cookies than any of the other scouts, too. Tomi liked to think up projects for her troop, and when war was declared, she'd suggested they learn to knit and make socks for the soldiers. All the girls went to the Itano house to learn knitting from Mom, who was good at knitting and sewing. Tomi wanted Mom to be a scout leader, but Mom was too shy.

Tomi was proud of her green uniform and yellow scarf. She ironed it every week so that it was fresh for the after-school meeting. She and Martha always walked to the Malkin house together on Girl Scout days.

As they reached the porch, Mrs. Malkin came outside and stood in front of the screen door, blocking their way. Mary Jane was beside her. "Go on in, Martha," she said.

Martha paused a moment, looking at Tomi, but Mrs. Malkin opened the door. "I told you to go inside, Martha."

Martha glanced at Tomi and did as she was told, but she stood just inside the screen. Tomi started to follow, but Mrs. Malkin put her hand on the door and held it closed. "I'm sorry, Tomi, but you're not welcome here anymore."

Tomi didn't understand. She tried to recall if she had done something wrong. Maybe she'd forgotten to wear her uniform or she'd failed to complete the work for a merit badge, but those things wouldn't have kept her from attending a meeting. She turned to Mary Jane, who was standing next to her mother, but her friend wouldn't look at her. Instead, Mary Jane rubbed the toe of her shoe back and forth on the porch floor.

"Why? What did I do?" Tomi asked.

Mrs. Malkin looked uncomfortable then. "It's best that you not be a scout anymore. I'm sorry." She didn't sound sorry to Tomi.

"Why? Why can't I be a scout anymore?"

"This is an American troop."

Tomi looked at Mrs. Malkin. "I'm an American. I was born right here in California, before you moved here from Ohio."

"We don't allow Japs in this house," Tomi heard Mr. Malkin say. She'd never liked him much. He expected Pop to give him a discount on strawberries, and whenever the scouts had a family potluck, he took more than his share of Mom's Japanese food.

"Don't be difficult, Tomi. That's the way things are," Mrs. Malkin told her.

"That's not fair," Martha said through the screen. "Tomi can't help who she is. She's the best scout in the whole troop. You can't ask her to leave."

Mrs. Malkin looked back at Martha. "Be still. This does not concern you, Martha. You're too young to understand."

"I do so understand. Maybe I don't want to be a scout

if Tomi can't. Come on, Tomi, let's go home."

Tomi shook her head. If Martha quit, that would only make things worse. Tomi heard the other scouts whispering behind the door and knew they would blame Tomi. They would tell everyone at school that Martha's leaving was Tomi's fault. "No, you stay," Tomi whispered. She turned quickly, so that no one would see the tears in her eyes. She wished she were so small she could disappear. She wouldn't run, though. Instead, she forced herself to walk at a normal pace until she turned the corner and was out of sight. Then when no one could see her, Tomi broke into a run and didn't stop until she reached home. There she ripped off her yellow Girl Scout scarf and threw it into the stove.

The next week on Girl Scout day, Tomi wore a regular dress. Mom didn't ask why. She knew.

★

Although Mr. Lawrence talked to a lawyer, there wasn't anything that could be done about Pop. The lawyer explained that the government had passed wartime laws that allowed it to keep men in prison when they were only *suspected* of being spies. There didn't have to be proof.

A few weeks after Pop was taken away, Mom received a letter from him, saying he had been sent to New Mexico. There were no details, because most of the letter was blacked out. There wasn't even a return address, so Mom couldn't write him—or visit him. But they couldn't have done that anyway, because they had been told they couldn't go more than five miles from their home. And they weren't allowed to be out after dark, either.

By then, the government was asking all Japanese living on the West Coast to move away from the ocean—to Montana and Colorado and Kansas, where they would be too far away to contact the Japanese enemy. Mom refused. How would Pop ever find them if they left California? she asked. Besides, they couldn't just walk away from the farm Pop had worked so hard to make successful. Roy volunteered to quit school so that he could take Pop's place with the strawberries, but Mom wouldn't let him. "Pop wants you to finish high school, because he didn't have that opportunity in Japan," she told him.

Even if Roy had quit school, it wouldn't have made a difference, because in February, just two months after Pearl Harbor was bombed, the government issued

Executive Order 9066. The order allowed the government
to round up all Japanese people living on the West Coast
and send them to ten "relocation camps" in California,
the mountain states, and Arkansas. Roy scoffed at that.
"Relocation, heck! They're sending us to prison."

★

In April, the government notified the Itanos that they
had just two weeks to get ready to move. They would be
allowed to take with them only what would fit into their
suitcases. That meant just clothes and underwear, a table-
cloth, a little bedding, maybe a few personal items such as
photographs. There wouldn't be time to harvest the crop.
Mom was frantic. "Who'll take care of the strawberries?"
she asked Mr. Lawrence. "They'll die."

"I'll find someone. Don't you worry about that, Mrs.
Itano," he said.

"But what about our things? We can take so little.
What will happen to our furniture, my china, the refrig-
erator?"

Mr. Lawrence thought that over. "If I can't find anybody to rent the place, I don't have any way to protect the

house after you leave, and who knows how long you'll be away. I'm afraid anything you leave behind could be stolen. You'd better sell what you can. There are men out there who will buy everything."

Later that day, Mrs. Lawrence came to the Itano house with Martha and said, "I can store some of your things, your china and silver, at our place. I wish there was room for the big items, but there isn't."

Tomi helped pack up the dishes and plates Mom had brought from Japan, the silverware Pop had bought her for her birthday, and the Philco radio, which Roy had fixed after the FBI men tore it apart. The government men had told them they weren't to take any radios with them. Or cameras or flashlights either.

As Martha and Mrs. Lawrence got into their car with the boxes, Tomi came out of the house holding Janice, the doll her *Baba* had sent her from Japan. Mom had said there wasn't room in the suitcase for the doll, and it had to be left behind. "Will you take care of Janice for me, Martha?" Tomi asked. When they were younger, the two girls had played dolls together, Martha with her blonde doll that looked like the movie star Shirley Temple and Tomi with the Japanese doll.

Martha smoothed her dress, then reached for the doll and set it carefully in her lap. "Janice will be waiting when you get back," she said.

Later that day, a man who ran a second-hand store came to the door and said he'd buy the Itanos' furniture.

"At least we won't have to give things away," Mom told Tomi. She showed the man through the house, telling him what the Itanos had paid for the sofa, the beds, the kitchen table.

"I'll give you five dollars for all of it," the man said.

"Five dollars?" Mom shrieked. "The sofa cost twenty-five, and it's only two years old."

The man shrugged. "It's better than nothing, lady."

Roy, who'd heard the man, was angry. "For five dollars, I'd burn it all up," he said.

"Seven dollars then. That's my final offer."

"Get out," Roy said, pointing to the door.

"Suit yourself," the man said and left.

Other people came to the Itano house after that, hoping to buy things cheaply. Their offers weren't much higher, but Mom knew she had to take what she could get. And so she sold the sofa for five dollars, the beds for two dollars each, the kitchen table and chairs for a dollar. The kitchen curtains went for ten cents, and Mom sold her silk scarves for a nickel.

The highest offer for her washing machine was twenty-five cents, and Mom refused it. The washing machine was her pride. It had a wringer—two rolls operated by a crank that squeezed the water out of the clothes after they'd been washed.

"Maybe you better take the quarter for the machine," Roy told Mom the day before they were to leave.

"No!" Mom said. "Nobody gets my washing machine for a quarter." She went out to the shed and brought back Pop's hammer. "I'll smash it before I sell it for twenty-five cents." Mom raised the hammer and broke one of the rollers. Then she hit the crank until it fell off. Roy began to laugh and took the hammer from her. He smashed the inside of the machine. When he was finished he handed the hammer to Tomi, who dented the sides, then turned the hammer over to Hiro. He chipped away at the enamel. When they were finished, the washing machine looked as if it had fallen off a truck.

Mom stood back, her hands over her mouth, as if she were ashamed of what they'd done. But then she began to laugh, maybe the first time she'd laughed since Pop had been taken away by the FBI a few weeks before. "There, that will show *them*."

She didn't say who *them* was, but Tomi knew. *Them* was all those people out there who thought the Itano family was their enemy. None of them were going to use Mom's washing machine.

1942 | CHAPTER FOUR
A HORSE-STALL HOTEL

EARLY one morning, Mr. Lawrence picked up the Itanos in his truck, which used to be Sam's. Mom had sold it to him for a hundred dollars, five times what the used-car lot had offered her. The Itanos had been told to report to a church in town. With their heavy suitcases, they would have had trouble walking all that distance if Mr. Lawrence hadn't offered to drive them.

Mom wore pants. Tomi had never seen her wear slacks before. The clothing and bedding they were taking with them had been crammed into the suitcases. In addition, Mom carried a shopping bag with her teapot and cups, both the everyday cups and her good ones. She was taking them with her because "it would never be home without them," she said, as she wrapped them in pillowcases and underwear to keep them from breaking.

"Martha wanted to come, but I told her it would be too crowded," Mr. Lawrence said, as he helped Tomi into the bed of the truck. Tomi was glad Martha wasn't there. She would have been embarrassed if her friend had seen her and her family looking like this. Hiro and Roy climbed up beside Tomi, and Mr. Lawrence handed up the bags. Then he opened the truck door for Mom. She glanced back at the house, as if she might not ever see it again. She was proud of that house, and she and Tomi had scrubbed it until it shone, because that's the way Japanese did things, Mom said. Being Americans, she told Tomi, didn't mean they had to forget their Japanese values. "If Mr. Lawrence finds someone to rent it, I would be shamed if the house was dirty. It is like when migratory birds leave a lake. They move smoothly and do not make the water murky. We will not leave this house murky."

"There's a box of lunch on the seat there," Mr. Lawrence told her. "Mrs. Lawrence was afraid they might forget to feed you on the bus."

Mom's voice was quiet when she said her thanks. Then she asked, "You'll tell Sam where we are, won't you? When he comes back, you'll say we wanted to wait for him, but we couldn't wait any longer, won't you?"

"Of course I will, Sumiko," Mr. Lawrence replied, as if he hadn't reassured her a dozen times already.

"Well, here we go," Roy said, as the truck bounced onto the road. "You know what they call us? *Evacuees.* That's because we have to *evacuate.*"

"What's that mean?" Hiro asked.

"It means 'leave.' "

Roy tried to sound jolly, but Tomi wouldn't have it. The metal bed of the truck was cold against her legs, and she shivered. "Where are we going?"

"Beats me. They haven't had time to build the camps yet. Maybe they'll send us to a hotel, a big one with a swimming pool," Roy said.

But Tomi was sure there wouldn't be a big hotel.

They were quiet then, not talking until Mr. Lawrence stopped in front of the church. A crowd of other evacuees was waiting. Like the Itanos, they wore layers of clothing and carried suitcases and boxes tied with rope. Soldiers with guns watched them.

Mr. Lawrence helped them unload their bags. He took off his hat and took Mom's hands. She looked down at them for a moment. Then she said, "If Sam comes—"

"I'll tell him," Mr. Lawrence said one more time. He shook hands with Roy, got back in the truck, and left.

Mom looked confused. "I wish your father was here. I wonder what we do," she said. Because Mom was shy, Pop had always taken care of everything.

"I'll find out," Roy told her, but Mom put up her hand.

"I think maybe I'm supposed to be in charge. I think that's what Pop would want. Things are different now," she said. That wasn't like Mom, and Tomi and Roy exchanged glances. Mom looked around, then slowly walked toward a soldier. She stood there politely until the soldier looked down at her. He pointed to a man standing beside the church entrance, and Mom disappeared into the crowd.

"I better go help her," Roy said.

Tomi touched his arm. She knew that Mom wanted to do this on her own, and she shook her head. "Let's see what happens."

They waited, and after a while, Mom returned with tags in her hand. "They gave us a family number. We are to put it on our bags and even on us. Then we can get on the bus." When the tags were attached to the suitcases and the coats, the Itanos made their way to one of the buses, waving at people they recognized. Tomi smiled at a boy she knew from school, and she heard a girl whisper, "Holy Smoke! That's Roy Itano. He's one of the Jivin' Five."

Roy nudged Tomi as they boarded the bus. "Hear that? This relocation business might not be so bad after all." He patted his bag, which contained his clarinet.

When they were seated, Hiro asked where they were headed. Mom shrugged, but Roy said he'd heard they were going to Santa Anita.

"The racetrack?" Tomi asked.

Roy nodded, and Hiro said, "That'd be swell! Maybe they'll let me ride a horse."

"No horses," Roy told him.

"Where will they put us? They must have a big hotel," Mom said.

Tomi thought that over and decided there wouldn't be a hotel large enough for all the people who were being sent to relocation camps. All the way to Santa Anita, Tomi worried about where they would sleep.

She found out when they arrived at the racetrack, which was surrounded by a high barbed-wire fence. Soldiers with guns stood along the fence and watched from guard towers. The Itanos were given a room number and sent to a stable. Maybe they'd live in one of the jockeys' rooms, Roy said. But as they walked down the aisle between the stalls, Tomi realized that wouldn't happen. The Itanos had been assigned a small cubicle—a horse stall! Mom stepped inside the small enclosure and looked around. There was fresh straw on the floor, and the walls had been whitewashed. "They didn't do a very good job of cleaning first," Tomi observed. She wrinkled her nose and made a face. There was the smell of horses and manure, too. "How can we live like this?" she asked.

"We can't," Roy said. "There's been a mistake. I'll find out what's going on."

"No mistake," Mom said. "Did you see the tents on the racetrack? This is better."

"A horse stall, Mom?" Tomi asked.

"*Shikata ga nai,*" Mom said. "It cannot be helped. We will make the best of our horse-stall hotel."

★

They left their belongings in the stall and went outside, where people were lined up at the entrances to tents and crude buildings. "I think that's the dining room," Roy said, pointing to a long building made of unpainted lumber. He had found a friend who told him what was going on. "And those buildings are for the men's and women's latrines."

"You have to wait in line to go to the bathroom?" Hiro asked.

"And to take a shower. There isn't any bathroom in our horse-stall hotel," Roy told him.

"We must see about supper," Mom said. "It will be nice not to have to cook for a change."

Tomi knew Mom was trying to look on the good side of things, because she loved to cook.

They waited in line for a long time, almost an hour, before they entered a room filled with tables and long benches. At one table, men served food they dished up from big pots and dumped onto tin plates. When a man handed Tomi her plate, she wrinkled her nose in disgust at the hot dog. She'd never liked hot dogs. "Since everybody here's Japanese, I thought we'd have Japanese food," she said.

"There's rice," Hiro told her. Then he examined his own plate. "I think there are flies in the rice."

Tomi studied the rice on her plate. "Raisins. Those are raisins."

"Who would put raisins in rice?"

"Somebody who doesn't know Japanese people," Tomi replied.

Mom looked around for a place where her family could sit. The tables were crowded, and there were spaces only here and there.

"I guess we have to eat by ourselves," Tomi said. She spotted a single space next to the boy she recognized from school and headed for it. She didn't see the frown on Mom's face.

★

Over the next few weeks and months, Tomi grew used to the horse-stall hotel. She and Mom shared a mattress tick filled with straw, sleeping under a rough blanket. Roy and Hiro shared one, too. Mom had brought sheets, but there was no place to wash them or hang them up to dry. Besides, the days and nights were so hot that after a while, they slept without any covering. Tomi missed the farm, the fresh strawberries and lettuce and corn. Most of all, she missed Pop. She remembered standing next to him when he raised the flag.

They spent only their nights in the horse stall, because

with the heat, the stable smelled even worse. Besides, there was nothing to do in the stall. Tomi became friends with some of the girls her age. They made toys for the younger children—dolls from worn-out socks and sticks or puzzles from magazine pictures, which they cut into shapes. She wondered if they could form a Girl Scout troop. After all, they were all Japanese, so none of them would be asked to leave because they weren't Americans. But they would all be moving on soon, to different relocation camps.

One day, one of the guards told Roy some friends had come to see him—the other members of the Jivin' Five. Roy was surprised, because gas was being rationed. Each family was allowed only a few gallons of gasoline each month. Roy said he liked it that his friends used some of their gasoline to drive to the racetrack to visit him.

"Can I come with you?" Tomi asked.

"Nah, this is just for guys," he said.

She watched him hurry away, then was surprised when he returned not more than thirty minutes later. He looked angry, and Tomi thought his eyes glistened with tears. "What's wrong? How come your friends didn't stay longer?" she asked.

"I told them to go on home. I don't want them to visit

anymore."

"Why? Is it because you're Japanese?"

Roy shook his head.

"Were they mean?"

"No, they were all right. They brought me some sheet music."

"Then what happened?"

Roy took his sister's hand. "It was awful. I had to talk to them through a *barbed-wire fence!*"

1942 | CHAPTER FIVE

TALLGRASS

FINALLY, in August, after four months of living in the racetrack, the Itanos received an order to move again. Mom didn't want to go. She wondered how Pop would ever find them.

Tomi was glad, however, because she was tired of living in a smelly horse stall and playing in the dirt of the racetrack.

"Where's our camp going to be?" she asked Roy, who only shrugged and said nobody knew. The guards would tell them when they got there, he said, as they boarded the train with other evacuees. Tomi had never ridden a train before and was excited. But the train was as hot as the stable at Santa Anita. People weren't allowed to get off when the train stopped at stations or even go out onto the observation platforms. And they couldn't open the windows. In fact, they were told they must keep the shades pulled down for the entire trip.

"Are they afraid people will see us or we'll see people?" Roy asked a guard. Just like Santa Anita, the train was filled with guards carrying guns. The soldier only shook his head. He didn't know. After Roy talked with another guard, he came back to his seat and whispered to Tomi, "He thinks we're going to Tallgrass. That's the camp in Colorado."

"I've read about Colorado," Tomi said. "They have mountains and rivers and big pine trees, and it snows there." None of the Itanos had ever seen snow. "I wouldn't mind Colorado," she added. Her spirits lifted, and for the first time since she left her house in California, Tomi thought the relocation might be an adventure.

After days, the train stopped and the evacuees were told to gather their belongings. They were at their destination. Tomi was so excited that she pushed to the front of the car so that she could be one of the first ones off. She jumped down onto the platform and looked around, then stopped. The station was in a dusty town set in the middle of the prairie. Dirt blew across the streets, and everything was brown. Where were the mountains? The snow? The tall pines? "This can't be Colorado," she told Hiro when he caught up with her. She squinted in the harsh sunlight.

"What is this place?" a man called to a crowd of people who had gathered to see the evacuees arrive. Like Tomi, the other Japanese stared at the land around them, blinking in the bright sun.

"Ellis, Colorado," came the reply.

Ellis, Colorado, wasn't anything like California. There were no strawberry beds or lettuce fields. Tomi looked over at the crowd of people who had gathered at the station. Some of them stared curiously, but others were angry and called out mean things. "We don't want you Japs here," one man yelled.

"Go on back where you came from," called another.

Mom, who stood next to Tomi, whispered, "Don't they understand? We want to go back, but we can't. We don't want to be here."

Tomi saw a girl looking at her brown-and-white saddle shoes, and Tomi stared back at her. The two of them might have gone to the same school and been friends, she thought. But maybe the girl hated her for being Japanese. Maybe if Tomi was her classmate, the girl wouldn't allow her to be a Girl Scout. Dirt blew into her face, and Tomi took out her pink silk scarf and put it over her long black hair, tying it at the back of her neck. Then she joined Mom, Hiro, and Roy as they climbed onto one of the buses waiting near the train—buses that would take them to their new home.

They rode a mile down a dirt road, past fields of what a man said were sugar beets. Then they turned in at a gate. Tomi could tell from the barbed-wire fences and the guard towers that this was a prison camp, even though it was *called* a relocation camp. There was a sign over the gatehouse: "Tallgrass."

She could see that the camp wasn't ready for the evacuees. The barracks weren't finished. Many were missing doors and windows, and the ground was littered with lumber and wire. Nothing had been painted. There were no gardens or sidewalks, only dirt. Tomi listened to the sounds of the carpenters, the talk of the people as they got off the buses. She looked at the long rows of barracks and the dirt streets. The camp wasn't pretty.

But it would be, Tomi thought suddenly. The Japanese she knew in California had been good gardeners. They would plant trees and flowers and vegetable gardens. Some would create rock gardens. The women would hang curtains in the windows. There would be schools and shops. Before long, Tallgrass would be a regular town, and each person in it would be like her, an American whose ancestors were Japanese. Tallgrass really was going to be an adventure, she thought. She turned to Hiro and said, "It looks like we're home."

★

If Mom was upset by their living space, she didn't show it. Their "apartment," as it was called, was just one room, sixteen by twenty feet. That was only a little larger than their living room in California. The unpainted walls were so thin that Tomi could hear people talking in the apartment next door. There was just one window, and a single lightbulb hung from the ceiling. A coal-burning stove stood in the center of the room. Except for cots with thin mattresses, there was no furniture.

Roy bit his lip as he dropped two suitcases on the floor. "They expect us to live here, all four of us?"

"Better than the horse place," Mom said.

"But this is permanent, Mom. We might be here a long

time," Roy argued.

"I like it," Mom said, although she didn't sound so sure.

Shikata ga nai, it can't be helped, Tomi thought. Mom smiled at Tomi and took a deep breath. "A small place, not so much cleaning to do."

"Plenty of dusting," Roy told her, rubbing his hand across the window sill, then examining it. Dust was already blowing in through a crack in the wall onto the suitcases. Roy slapped his hands together, then grabbed Hiro's arm. "Come on, let's get out of here and find out where the mess hall is." The two of them left, Roy slamming the door so hard that the walls shook.

Mom stared at the door, then straightened her back. "Good. They won't be in the way. Let's set up our new home, Tomi. First thing, find a broom. Too much dust and sawdust on the floor."

They hadn't brought a broom with them, of course, and Tomi didn't know where to look for one. She went outside and searched until she spotted a pile of lumber—with a broom on top. One of the workmen must have thrown it away, because the top half of the broomstick had broken off. Still, Tomi was as excited as if she'd found a silver dollar lying on the ground. She snatched it up and returned to the apartment.

"Such good luck!" Mom said when Tomi showed her the broom. "With the stick broken, the broom is just the right size for you. You sweep, I'll dust, and then we will unpack." So while Mom dusted the walls and the cots with a dish towel she had brought with her, Tomi swept the floor. She wet a newspaper she'd taken from the trash pile, then dropped clumps of it onto the floor so that the dirt would stick to the paper as she pushed it around with the broom. Then the two shoved the suitcases against a wall and opened them. Mom took out a sheet and held it up. "If they don't give us a wall for a bedroom, we'll make our own," she said. "Roy can figure out how to hang the sheet. Our cots will be on one side, theirs on the other."

Tomi went to her suitcase and took out a pretty yellow-flowered skirt. Mom had made it for her, using three yards of material. "This would make curtains," Tomi said. "I could tear out the hem and open up the waistband. We brought needles and thread. I could sew the curtains by hand." Mom's sewing machine had been sold for a dollar.

"A good idea," Mom told her. "First we make up a table."

"But we don't have a table," Tomi said.

"We will use the stove. Who needs a stove to heat the room in August?"

Tomi hummed as she and Mom took out the table-cloth, folded it, and placed it on top of the stove. Mom had never before asked her to help arrange a room. They unpacked the teapot and cups and Tomi placed them on the tablecloth. Mom stood back and admired the arrange-ment. "All we need is a vase of flowers."

"I'll go pick them," Tomi said, and they both laughed. There were no flowers growing in this dry dirt!

By the time Hiro and Roy returned, Tomi and Mom had unpacked the suitcases. Tomi had picked up a handful of bent nails from the pile of discarded lumber and used the heel of her shoe to pound them into the wall. And now the four of them hung the clothes on the nails. "You see, we don't have to go through a closet to choose our clothes. They are right there on the wall where we can see them," Mom said.

"But I only have two shirts, and I'm wearing one," Hiro pointed out.

"Even easier," Mom said. She turned to Roy. "There are knotholes in the wall. You can see sunlight through them. That's why there's so much dust. You find a cook and tell him we want tin can lids to nail over the holes."

Tomi didn't know why Mom seemed so happy. Maybe it was that they were finally away from the racetrack, or perhaps it was that she was settling into a "home." She couldn't stop the family from being evacuated, but she and Tomi could arrange the room any way they wanted.

It struck Tomi then that Mom had changed a little just in the months since Pop was arrested. She had always done what everyone else wanted. Now for the first time in her life, she was in charge. Maybe something good had come from the evacuation. It wasn't much. Were there other good changes? Tomi would look for them.

1942 | CHAPTER SIX
RICE *and* FRUIT COCKTAIL

THE food wasn't much better at Tallgrass than it had been at Santa Anita. There was something called Spam that came in a can and was sliced and fried. Tomi thought the bottom of her shoe would taste better. The only fish was tuna fish, which came from a can, too. Instead of fresh vegetables, there were canned beans and peas. And dessert was rice with syrupy fruit cocktail poured over it.

"This is not good food. I will talk to the cooks about it," Mom said as she looked over her plate of macaroni and cheese.

"You will?" Hiro asked.

Tomi shoved him with her elbow. She liked this new Mom. The old one never would have complained, but now Mom was quick to tell someone in charge when things were wrong. She demanded lumber so that Roy could build shelves in their apartment and a table and chairs. She complained about the bathrooms. "Ladies need privacy," she said, after she visited the latrine. The toilets were in a big room, with no partitions around them. Some women carried pieces of cardboard to screen themselves.

"Mom's different. She never used to say a word. Now she's pushy," Roy said, as they looked around for places to sit in the mess hall. Dinner had always been a family affair in California. They ate together, and no one missed supper unless there was a good reason. But now, as at Santa Anita, the evacuees sat at different tables, the children with their friends, the older people with each other.

"She's more like Pop," Tomi replied. "With him gone, she's in charge."

"Well, *I'm* supposed to be in charge. I'm the man now." Roy spotted a seat next to a girl he had met on the train and started for it.

"You can't be in charge. Boys your age just care about pretty girls," Tomi told him.

"What's wrong with that?" Roy grinned. "Maybe I'll start up a dance band, and then I'll have plenty of them falling all over me."

"But if you play in the band, you won't be able to dance with them," Tomi pointed out.

While Roy headed for the vacant seat, Tomi looked around the room and spotted a seat next to a girl she'd seen come out of the barracks just down from where the Itanos lived. She made her way to the table and sat down.

"Hi," she said, but the girl only nodded and stared at her plate.

"I'm Tomi. If you'll be my friend, I'll give you my yummy rice," Tomi joked.

The girl looked up at Tomi then and giggled, putting her hand over her mouth. "You can't trick me. I think it's the worst rice I ever had."

"Me, too." Tomi laughed. "You want my hot dog?"

"No."

The two laughed again. "Tonight we're going to have Spam *tempura*," the girl said. *Tempura* was a Japanese way of coating seafood or vegetables with a light batter, then deep-frying it.

"That's a good one! My brother thinks they use flies instead of raisins in the rice pudding," Tomi said, laughing.

Before long, the two were talking as if they'd known each other their whole lives.

"I'm Ruth Hayashi," the girl introduced herself. "I've seen you. You're in the building with the yellow curtains."

"That's our apartment. I made them out of a skirt."

"You can sew?"

Tomi nodded. "My mother taught me."

"She sews too? I bet my mom can't even thread a needle. We always had somebody who did our sewing for us," Ruth said.

Tomi couldn't imagine a woman who didn't sew. Then she studied Ruth for a moment. The girl was wearing a silk dress and patent-leather shoes. A pearl necklace was around her neck. Tomi asked where Ruth had come from.

"San Francisco. My dad had a company that imported things from Japan—jade, pearls, carved wooden boxes. He had to sell it when we were evacuated. We used to be rich. Now ..." Ruth shrugged.

"Nobody's rich in here," Tomi said.

"That means Mother can't hire anyone to do her work. She's never even swept a floor. Good thing we have a mess hall, because she can't cook either."

Tomi had heard about rich Japanese women who sat on silk cushions all day. She'd thought that would be a wonderful life, never having to wash dishes or pick strawberries.

But suddenly, she felt sorry for Ruth and her mother. The camp must be awful for them. She and Mom were adjusting to Tallgrass because they had worked hard all their lives. They knew how to clean the apartment and wash clothes. They'd lived on a farm and understood how the wind picked up dirt and blew it into buildings.

Mom had been smart to take slacks and sturdy shoes to wear at Tallgrass. Tomi imaged Ruth's mother wearing high heels and silk clothes. What would they do when winter came? She'd read about snow in Colorado.

"I could teach you to sew," Tomi said. "It's not hard."

"You could?" Ruth looked down at her fragile dress, which was already torn. "Maybe you could teach me to mend, too."

Tomi had the beginning of an idea. "Maybe your mom could learn."

★

"Oh, Tomi, I couldn't teach anyone to sew," Mom said, when Tomi told her about Ruth and her mother.

"You taught me."

"That was different. You just told me about Mrs.

Hayashi being a high lady, and having servants."

"Not anymore," Tomi said. "I think they're just like us. Ruth said Mr. Hayashi sold his business."

"In Japan, someone like that wouldn't have anything to do with me."

"We're not in Japan, Mom," Tomi said. "We're in America." She glanced around the room at the crude furniture Roy had made, the tin can lids nailed over the knotholes in the wall, the sheet that screened Roy and Hiro's cots. "Well, maybe we're not even in America. We're in Tallgrass."

"No, I couldn't."

Tomi went to the window and looked out through the yellow curtains. Someone in the barracks across from her had collected rocks and arranged them into a nice display. "You complained about the latrines and the food. You helped women that way. What's wrong with helping just one learn to sew? I think Pop would want you to."

"Don't you tell me what Pop wants," Mom said quickly. "I'm trying hard enough on my own to do that."

Tomi turned around and looked at her mom. "I'm sorry."

Mom sighed. Then she went to the window. "Is that Mrs. Hayashi?" She pointed to a woman in a wrinkled silk dress and high-heeled shoes making her way past the apartment. When Tomi nodded, Mom said, "She looks very tired. And dirty."

"Ruth says she doesn't know how to wash clothes, and when she went to the wash room, nobody would help her. Ruth says people don't mix with her because she used to be rich."

"That's not right," Mom said. She sighed and turned away from the window. "It's wrong to judge people that way. We were sent to this camp because people who didn't even know us thought we were bad. I would not want to be like them. You must invite Ruth and her mother for tea."

"Here?"

"Of course here." Mom went to the coal stove and removed the teapot and cups, then the tablecloth. They would find scraps of lumber and build a fire, then heat water in a pan on top of the stove. "They will be our first guests," Mom said.

1943 | CHAPTER SEVEN
POOR MRS. HAYASHI

TOMI was getting used to the camp now that she had been there for more than four months. She missed California, of course. She missed the lush fields, the strawberries still fresh with morning dew that she could pick for breakfast. And most of all, she missed being able to go where she wanted. In California, she could run for blocks, for miles even. But Tallgrass was all dirt streets, and the camp was enclosed by barbed wire. Guards in towers watched the evacuees, even the children. They were afraid to play near the fence, although the guards didn't threaten them. Sometimes they even gave the children gum and Hershey bars.

There were things she liked about the camp. There were no strawberries to weed and pick and box, no dishes to wash. Housekeeping was only a little dusting and sweeping. Of course, it had to be done two or three times a day, since despite the tin can lids nailed over cracks in the walls, the dirt still blew in. There was the laundry to do, too. Tomi and Mom went to the wash house every week with dirty clothes. They scrubbed clothes in the sinks, then hung them up to dry, hoping the dirt didn't blow onto their wet clothes. Still, those duties were easy, and Tomi had plenty of time left over to play.

What Tomi liked best was school, which had opened late in the fall of 1942. At first, Japanese men and women volunteered to teach, but after a time, trained teachers were hired from outside. The school wasn't much at first—tables instead of desks, no textbooks, not even a blackboard. Still, Tomi loved it. Her favorite subject was English. She looked forward to the stories the teacher read at the end of the day, and she liked writing her own stories, too. She kept her handwriting small, filling up each page with as many words as she could, because paper was scarce.

Ruth was in Tomi's class, and each morning, Tomi and Hiro stopped to pick her up on their way to school.

"You're lucky your dad's here in the camp," Tomi told Ruth one day, as Mr. Hayashi waved to them from the doorway of the barracks. "I wish they'd send Pop to Tall-grass."

"Me, too," Hiro said, and Tomi realized how much her brother missed their father. He'd been sent away nearly a year before.

"Do they let him write you letters?" Ruth asked. Tomi had told her that Pop was being held in a prison in New Mexico.

"He writes them, but we can't read them," Tomi replied. "Somebody blacks out every other word, so most of the time, we don't know what he's talking about. I guess he's okay, but he doesn't seem very happy. At home, Pop was always having a good time. He made everybody laugh. But not anymore. I think that's because he misses us."

"Why is he in prison?" Ruth asked.

Tomi shrugged. "We don't know. The government hasn't filed any charges against him. It seems like he's being held there just because he's Japanese."

"It must be hard for your mom."

"She tries to hide her feelings, but I've seen her cry when she thinks I'm not watching," Tomi said. "It's not fair."

Ruth agreed. Then she added, "It's not fair my brother

died, either."

At that, Tomi stopped and stared at her friend. "You had a brother? You never told me about him."

"I miss him as much as you do your dad. His name was Ben. Father doesn't want me to talk about him, so I never do. It makes Mother sad."

"What happened?"

Ruth scraped the toe of her shoe in the dirt and looked away. "He had a sickness. I don't know what it was. He had it a long time. We could have hired a nurse, but Mother said she wanted to take care of him. So that's what she did all day and sometimes all night." When Ruth saw Tomi staring at her, she added, "Mother isn't lazy. I mean, she can't cook or sew or clean, but she spent all of her time with Ben. She gave up parties and helping at the store and everything else to be with him." Ruth looked down at the dirt and kicked at a rock. "Father said Ben lived as long as he did because Mother took such good care of him."

"How old was he?"

"Younger than me. Ben was four when he died. That was last year. He was sick for two years. Without Ben, it's like there's a hole in our lives." Ruth blinked as she started down the street toward school. "Don't mention him to

P O O R   M R S .   H A Y A S H I

Mother. She'll cry. Like I said, we don't ever talk about him. That's why I never told you."

Tomi remembered then that she had gone into the Hayashis' apartment one day and saw Mrs. Hayashi holding a toy dog. It was on wheels and there was a string to pull it back and forth. Mrs. Hayashi had been rolling the wheels across her hand, but she put the toy behind her back when she saw Tomi. Tomi thought it was odd that Mrs. Hayashi had brought one of Ruth's baby toys to the camp, but now she realized the toy dog had belonged to Ben. Mrs. Hayashi wouldn't leave it behind, even though it had taken up precious space in her suitcase. Tomi wondered if Mrs. Hayashi had brought other things that had been Ben's.

"Maybe your mom will have another brother for you one day, or a sister," Tomi said.

Ruth shrugged. "I wish. Mother just sits in the room all day holding Ben's things. Everybody thinks she's unhappy because Father sold his business and we're living in the camp. But it's really because she misses Ben." She took Tomi's hand. "Come on. We have to hurry. Remember, the Boy Scouts are going to come to our class today."

Tomi tried to think about the visitors to the school

then, but her mind kept slipping back to Ruth's mother. Tomi's father had gone away, and she missed him more than anything in the world. But she knew he would come back one day. Poor Mrs. Hayashi. Ben would never return.

1943 | CHAPTER EIGHT
MAKING FRIENDS *with the* ENEMY

THE Boy Scouts from Ellis arrived just after class started. Their scoutmaster had visited the Tallgrass school the week before to make the arrangements for the scouts to attend class and eat lunch. His wife, Mrs. Glessner, was Tomi's teacher, which was why the scouts were visiting Tomi's class. She'd heard Mr. Glessner tell his wife that maybe if the children got to know each other, they'd realize they weren't that different. He'd said they would develop a tolerance the adults didn't have. Tomi asked Roy what "tolerance" meant, and he told her it meant respect and understanding. That made Tomi think about Mrs. Malkin, her Girl Scout leader at home. Mrs. Malkin didn't have tolerance.

The Boy Scouts marched into the room that morning

and lined up against the wall. They were older than Tomi. Some wore their scout shirts. Others were dressed in regular clothes, and Tomi wondered if maybe they couldn't afford to buy uniforms. She hadn't thought about the Caucasians in Ellis being poor. Some of them might be as poor as the people in the camp.

Tomi and the other students stood politely as their guests entered the room, and several of the Japanese boys offered their seats on the benches to the visitors. But the scouts seemed embarrassed and stayed where they were, a few putting a foot against the wall to steady themselves.

"I think there is room on the benches for everyone if you crowd together," Mrs. Glessner said. The students sat back down and pushed to the middle of the benches, while the scouts found seats at the end. The two groups took quick glances at each other.

"Today, our history lesson is about the war in Europe," Mrs. Glessner said. "Who can tell me why we declared war on Germany?"

"Because the Japs bombed Pearl Harbor, and we don't like them. They're our enemy," a Boy Scout muttered. Another scout snickered.

Tomi felt the hair on her neck rise. The remark didn't

have anything to do with tolerance. Mr. Glessner was standing in the front of the room and said, "Dennis—"

But Mrs. Glessner interrupted. "That's not right. We declared war on the Japanese because they bombed Pearl Harbor, which is part of the United States, and the Germans are allies of the Japanese. 'Allies' means partners or friends. But that's not the only reason we went to war with Germany." She turned to Dennis. "And in this classroom, we use the word 'Japanese.' Calling someone a 'Jap' is as offensive as calling you a 'Kraut' because your father came from Germany."

"Hey, I'm an American," Dennis said.

"So are these students. We're all Americans here. Now, who can answer the question?" When no one answered, Mrs. Glessner looked around the room. "Tomi, can you tell us why we Americans declared war on Germany?" She emphasized the word "we."

Tomi felt her face turn red, and she looked down at the table. Why did Mrs. Glessner have to call on her? She wasn't the smartest one in the class. And she didn't like people looking at her. Maybe it was because she had written a story in class once about being an American. She glanced at Dennis to make sure he was listening, then said,

"*We Americans* went to war against Germany because Germany invaded other countries. *We Americans* are defending our friends."

"Very good," Mrs. Glessner said, then asked another question, but Tomi wasn't listening. Instead, she was watching Dennis, who had dropped his head until it almost reached the table.

Later, as she left the classroom to go to the dining hall for lunch, Tomi overheard Mrs. Glessner tell her husband, "I suppose I shouldn't have talked about the war. Maybe that was too much for the kids."

Mr. Glessner said, "Perhaps it was a good thing to get it all out in the open. After all, the camp is starting to issue daily passes so the Japanese kids can go into town. If the town kids can learn the children in the camp are just people, not enemies, they won't take them on. If we can stop just one bully, then it's worth it."

★

The evacuees were supposed to eat at the dining hall closest to their barracks, but there was a good deal of trying out the different mess halls to find which served the best food. The word would get out that a chef at another mess hall served Japanese food or had fish or fresh vegetables, and people would try the meals there. Although the cooks could do just so much with the food that was sent to the camp, they still competed with each other to see who could draw the biggest crowds.

Because the students didn't have much time for lunch, however, they usually ate at the dining hall closest to the school. The food there wasn't very good. That day there was a main dish of canned vegetables, bread, and rice with canned peaches poured over it.

Tomi was used to the food and didn't pay attention to it. She and Ruth found places at a table and sat down with their plates. As she picked up her fork, Tomi spotted that boy Dennis glancing around the dining hall. She nudged Ruth and asked if they should invite him to sit with them.

"He's looking for a place with white people. He wouldn't want to sit with us," Ruth said.

But Tomi caught Dennis's eye and waved and pointed to the seat next to her.

Dennis looked uncertain, but there were few other vacant places, so he put his plate on the table and sat down beside Tomi.

"You don't like us very much," she said.

Dennis shrugged. "You're Japs—*Japanese*," he corrected himself. "My dad thinks you ought to be shipped back to Japan."

"I've never been to Japan. Have you, Ruth?" Ruth shook her head. "I can't even speak Japanese," Tomi added. Then she asked slyly, "Can you speak German?"

"Sure. That's what we speak at home ..." Dennis's voice trailed off, and he looked at Tomi as if she'd pulled a fast one.

"Do you think you should go back to Germany? After all, America's fighting the Germans."

"No way," he said. "I'm a one-hundred-percent American."

"Me too."

"But you don't look like one."

"What do Americans look like?" Tomi asked.

"Like ..." Dennis made a helpless gesture. "Like me, I guess."

"Like Germans?"

"Well, we didn't get rounded up and sent to a camp."

"So we did because we don't look like you?"

Dennis shrugged. "I don't know. You're confusing me."

Tomi nodded. "I think everything about this camp is confusing."

Dennis looked down at the food on his plate. "The lunch doesn't look very good."

"It isn't," Ruth told him.

Dennis took a bit of the rice and made a face. "Who would put canned peaches on rice?"

"Somebody who doesn't have to eat it," Tomi told him.

Dennis laughed for the first time. Then he looked around the room at the people crowded about the tables. "This isn't much of a place. My dad read in the newspaper that you were eating steak and apple pie every day. The paper said you were living high on the hog and we were paying for it. It said the American government gave you all the sugar you wanted, while we don't get it because we're rationed. My mom can't even make jam, because the government lets her buy only a little bit of sugar."

Tomi laughed. "Look around. How much sugar do you see?"

"We haven't had dessert yet."

"That's what the rice and canned peaches are supposed to be."

Dennis made a face. "Okay, so you don't eat so good,

but what about your houses?"

"Barracks, you mean," Ruth said.

"Yeah. I guess you've got silk sheets and big carpets and radios."

"We don't even have linoleum floors, just wood," Tomi told him. "And they wouldn't let us bring radios with us. Or cameras. I guess somebody's afraid we'll take pictures of Ellis and send them to the Japanese government."

Dennis frowned. "Why would they care about Ellis? They're not dumb enough to bomb Ellis, are they?" Then he realized Tomi was teasing him, and he laughed again. In a minute, Ruth and Tomi joined him. After he stopped, Dennis said, "Hey, you're all right."

1943 | CHAPTER NINE
NEW NEIGHBORS

W H E N Tomi returned from school one afternoon, Roy told her a new family had moved into one of the apartments in their barracks. The old family had left the camp because the man had gotten a job working on a sugar beet farm.

Despite the barbed-wire fences and the guard towers, Tallgrass wasn't really a prison camp. The government moved the Japanese to Tallgrass and the other camps because it didn't want them living on the West Coast, where they might contact the enemy in Japan. But the evacuees weren't supposed to be permanent residents of the camps. The men were expected to get jobs, taking the places of those who had been drafted to fight in the war. In Colorado, the Japanese men were offered work on farms.

The women, too, could get jobs in cities at defense plants or as office workers. Once they found work, the evacuees would move out of the camps, and some at Tallgrass had already done so. Others found work in the sugar beet farms around Ellis and still lived at Tallgrass.

"Are there any kids?" Tomi asked, after Roy told her about the new family.

"Yeah, I think there's a boy Hiro's age."

"Yippee!" Hiro said, because his friends lived in other barracks. "Let's go meet them, Tomi."

The two went down the hall and knocked on the door of the new family's apartment. A girl about Roy's age opened the door. She was pretty, with long hair turned under, and she wore thick socks rolled down to her ankles, called bobby sox. Girls who wore them were called "bobby-soxers." She held the hand of a small boy about four years old, while a larger boy peered out from behind her.

"Hi," Tomi said, introducing the two of them. "We came to welcome you."

"Welcome?" the girl replied in an angry voice. "Why would anybody *welcome* us to this place?"

"I guess it's not so great, is it?" Tomi said.

"It's horrid. I hate being here. We were living in another barracks, but the roof leaked, so they sent us here. This is almost as bad. Look at the dirt."

"You have to dust every day, but it doesn't take long," Tomi said, trying to be cheerful.

The girl swept the dust off a chair and sat down, putting her hands over her face. "Dirt inside, dirt outside, everywhere you look there's dirt. And I haven't seen a single tree in the whole camp."

"No," Tomi admitted. "But some of the men are going to put in Japanese gardens, and my mom says she'll plant vegetables. It will be better."

"I don't care. I hate Tallgrass, and I hate the government for sending us here."

Just then, Hiro turned to the older boy and asked if he wanted to go outside and play. "When spring comes, we're starting a baseball team. Do you want to join?"

"Do I!" the boy replied. "I was the best catcher in my whole grade. My name's Wilson. Can I go outside, Helen?" he asked his sister.

"Might as well. There's nothing to do here," she told him.

As the two boys left, Tomi heard Wilson say, "Somebody told me you can hit a ball like Joe DiMaggio."

"Jeepers!" was all Hiro could say. Being compared to the great Yankee baseball player was the finest compliment anybody could give a little boy. Tomi knew Hiro had made a good friend.

"At least one of us is happy," Helen said bitterly. "What's here for me? It's not like I play baseball."

"Aren't you in school, or do you work?" Tomi asked.

"How can I do anything? I have to take care of Carl." She glanced at her little brother.

"What about your folks?"

"They're dead. Dad was killed in a fishing boat accident. Mom died of pneumonia just before we got sent to Colorado."

"At Santa Anita?" Tomi asked.

"A place like that, a fairground. There wasn't any hospital."

"I'm sorry. That must be hard."

"I hate America," Helen said.

Tomi glanced down at Carl. "You mean it's just you and your brothers? You're taking care of them all by yourself?"

Helen nodded.

"How old are you?"

"Sixteen."

"Don't you have any relatives who can help?"

Helen shook her head. "They're all in Japan. I wish I was there, too."

Tomi's mouth dropped open in surprise. "But Japan's our enemy. We're at war with Japan. We're Americans."

"I used to think that, too. I'm *Nisei*. That means I was born here. But look at the way this country treats us. If the government hadn't rounded us up and sent us to the fairground, my mother wouldn't have gotten sick. I'd be back in San Francisco going to school. Now I have to sit in this dirty room and take care of my brothers."

"I'm sorry," Tomi said, thinking "I'm sorry" didn't solve anything.

1943 | CHAPTER TEN
BUYING *a* TANK

R U T H was slumped in the doorway of her barracks when Tomi stopped on the way to the dining hall.

"I heard there's a cook on the other side of the camp who makes Japanese food for breakfast. We ought to go there sometime," Ruth said. "I'd give a quarter for just one bite of real Japanese food—that is, if I had a quarter."

"You know what I miss?" Tomi asked. "Strawberry ice cream. We used to make our own with fresh strawberries and cream from Mr. Lawrence's cows. We'd take turns turning the crank on the freezer. In the summer, we'd sit in the dark watching fireflies and eating ice cream."

"There's an ice cream parlor in Ellis. One of the Boy Scouts told me. Maybe in the summer, we can get passes to go there every day."

"That would be wonderful." Then Tomi remembered she had to hurry and grabbed Ruth's hand. "Come on. I promised Mom I'd come back and take her to that class. If I don't go with her, she might stay home. Mom doesn't like standing up in front of people. At home, she never spoke out when she was with white ladies. But I told her that here, everybody's Japanese."

Ruth nodded. "Ditto. My mom's shy, too. But she needs to get out. All she does is sit in the room and hold Ben's toys. Do you think this will work?"

"We have to try."

A couple of weeks before, when one of the women who taught at the camp saw the quilt Mrs. Hayashi was making with Mom's help, she'd asked Mom if she would teach a class in quilting. Mom said no, thank you, she wasn't good enough. That wasn't the real reason, however. Mom could sew anything. She turned down the request because she didn't want to get up in front of a group of women.

"You should, Mom. It's so cold in the winter at Tall-grass that people need quilts. And you can teach them just the way you did Mrs. Hayashi," Tomi told her.

"I couldn't," Mom said.

"That's selfish," Roy spoke up. He had been listening

in. "What if we needed warm quilts and somebody refused to teach you how to make them?"

Mom frowned. She said she wouldn't know any of the women in the class.

"You'll know Mrs. Hayashi," Tomi told her. "And me."

"You would go?"

Tomi thought that over. She'd spoken too quickly. She didn't want to sew with a bunch of women, but she'd go if it were necessary. She could always sneak out after Mom got started.

Now, the two girls ran down the street to the dining hall and joined the line waiting to get in. A girl from school motioned for the two girls to join her at the head of the line—"spacing" it was called. But Tomi knew that crowding in line was rude, so she shook her head, and she and Ruth waited their turn. It wasn't long, and they gobbled their lunch of canned spaghetti and raced back to the barracks.

When Tomi reached the room, she found Mom sitting on one of the rough chairs that Roy had made, her back very straight. Her hands were at the sides of her face, however, and she looked as if something was wrong.

"Come on, Mom, we're late. We're picking up Mrs.

Hayashi and Ruth. Mrs. Hayashi is scared to go. Can you imagine?" Tomi wondered if Ruth was telling Mrs. Hayashi that Mom was scared. "You know everybody," Tomi said to reassure her mother.

"That doesn't mean I can be a teacher."

"Sure you can."

Tomi wasn't so sure, however. Mom had come a long way since leaving the farm, but she was a woman who disliked being the center of attention. Mom forced herself to complain to the officials about things in the camp that were wrong. But that was because she was concerned about Tomi and Hiro and Roy. She'd never before agreed to stand up before other women as a teacher.

"You said you'd do it. So *shikata ga nai*. It can't be helped now." Tomi took Mom's hand. "Besides, you have to be there for Mrs. Hayashi. She won't go if you don't."

Mom nodded, and Tomi smiled to herself, because she knew Mom would not let down a friend.

Mrs. Hayashi was even more ill at ease than Mom when she left her apartment. Both women looked their best, with hats, and Mrs. Hayashi wore high-heeled shoes and even gloves. Still, they reluctantly followed their daughters down the street to one of the barracks buildings that had been turned into classrooms. "Maybe no one will come," Mom whispered to Mrs. Hayashi.

But the room was full of Japanese women who stood around a table talking. They were dressed up, too, as if this were an important occasion. When they saw Mom, they bowed and greeted her, some in English, some in Japanese. One woman had brought her daughter with her and said the girl could thread the needles.

Mom bowed back and said, "Hello. I am Mrs. Itano." Then, her hands shaking a little, she opened her paper sack and took out her scissors, needle, thread, and bits of fabric. "Welcome to our first quilting class. I am your teacher."

Tomi grinned at her. Mom was going to be all right.

Tomi watched as Mom told the ladies to take out the scraps of fabric they had brought. When Mom was busy examining the pieces, Tomi nodded at Ruth. They would slip away and play. But as she started for the door, she heard Mom's voice. "Tomi, stay please. Take a seat. You are going to be my star pupil."

Tomi sighed. She did not care about sewing, and she especially did not care about making quilts.

"We will each make a pieced quilt," Mom said. The ladies leaned forward to hear her. "Piecing is mostly squares and triangles." Mom held up a square of fabric and cut it on the diagonal, from upper right to lower left.

The ladies nodded their understanding.

Mom explained they would assemble the squares and triangles into a block. It would take many blocks to make a quilt.

"I don't have so much material," one lady complained.

Mom looked at the small stash of fabric the woman had brought, then glanced around the table. No one had enough for a quilt. She thought that over, then brightened. "I know. We will make one big quilt, all of us together."

"Who will get the quilt?" Mrs. Hayashi asked.

"Maybe we draw straws," another said.

"Yes," Mom said. "But it doesn't seem fair if we all work on the quilt and only one keeps it."

"We could give it to the hospital," Mrs. Hayashi suggested, and Mom nodded.

"I know," Tomi spoke up. "We can have a raffle. The money will go to the war effort."

The ladies smiled at each other and nodded. Mrs. Hayashi said, "It is a good idea. We can sell tickets for five cents. Maybe we will make enough money to buy a tank."

1943 | CHAPTER ELEVEN
SOLVING TWO PROBLEMS

A S T H E Y left the quilt room, Tomi told Ruth, "I don't think they'll make enough money to buy a tank; maybe only a gun."

"Who cares if it's only enough for a handful of bullets? This might be the first time I've seen Mother smile since Ben died," Ruth said.

Indeed, Mrs. Hayashi was smiling as she told Mom, "I think my husband has some indigo cloth from Japan left from the store. It is just cotton and was used to make work shirts a long time ago. The people who took over the business wanted only silk. The blue cotton is very old and very beautiful. I will ask my husband if the people in San Francisco will send it to us for a quilt." She took Mom's arm and smiled at her. "Perhaps we could make a Japanese design with your squares and triangles."

Then she asked if Tomi was going to help piece the quilt.

"Who, me?" Tomi asked and made a face. "I don't care about sewing. But I'll sell raffle tickets. Maybe everybody in camp will buy one. What's five cents times five thousand?"

"A lot," Ruth replied. "You know, I think quilting takes Mother's mind off Ben, at least for a little while. She seems happier when she's sewing. But other times ..." Ruth shrugged. Then she said, "I don't want to talk about Ben." She changed the subject. "Who's that new girl in your barracks? She looks familiar. She was standing in the hall when I came to your apartment yesterday, and she looked angry."

"You mean Helen," Tomi said. "She lives there with her two brothers. They're orphans. Her mom died just before Helen came to Tallgrass."

Ruth stopped and cocked her head. "Now I remember. I think I know her. She used to sing in the choir at our church in San Francisco. She's a bobby-soxer. She has a beautiful voice."

"She doesn't sing here. Mostly, she just looks mad,"

Tomi said.

"That's too bad. I was mad when I came here, but now, I'm not so mad. Does she work?" Many of the internees held jobs in the camp. They weren't paid much. Most received twelve to sixteen dollars a month to work in the post office or the print shop, where they produced posters for the war effort. Professional people, such as doctors, made only nineteen dollars. But the jobs filled their time and made the people feel useful. It also gave them a little money they could spend in the camp store or on items they sent away for in the Montgomery Ward catalogue. Mom was paid twelve dollars a month for teaching the quilting class, and she'd promised to spend her first paycheck on boots for Tomi.

"Helen doesn't work even though she's old enough to have a job. She doesn't go to school either. She has to take care of her little brother. She's like a mother to him. The camp was going to divide up the three of them and put them with different families, but Helen said no. She wouldn't give up her brothers," Tomi told Ruth. "It's not fair." She remembered that she had once told Ruth it wasn't fair that Pop was in prison, and Ruth had replied that it wasn't fair her brother, Ben, had died.

"There are a lot of things at Tallgrass that aren't fair."

The two hurried to catch up with their mothers when something occurred to Tomi. She put her hand on Ruth's arm, and the two stopped. "I have an idea ..."

Ruth looked at Tomi, a question on her face. "What?"

"I have an idea," Tomi repeated. "Your mother ..." She paused, thinking that what she was about to say was none of her business.

"My mother what?"

"Helen needs somebody to watch her brother Carl. He's four, the age you said Ben was when he died."

"And?"

Tomi took a deep breath. "What if your mother took care of him?"

"You mean you want her to work as a nursemaid? Mother would never do that. She's never worked a day in her life except for helping Father at the store. We could use the money, but Mother would think taking a job was ... well ... disgraceful. It would be as if she said Father couldn't provide for us and she had to help out. It would make Father feel useless."

"What if it's not a real job? Helen probably couldn't even pay her if she wanted to. Maybe your mother could just 'help out.' With your brother gone, she might like having Carl around."

Ruth looked down at the ground, thinking. "I don't know," she said at last.

"You could ask her," Tomi said.

Ruth shook her head. "She'd say no, just like your mother did the first time she was asked to teach the quilting class. We'd have to find another way. We'd have to make her think it was her idea."

"We could just take Carl to meet her, and maybe she'd get the idea on her own," Tomi suggested.

Ruth slowly nodded her head up and down. "I don't know if that will work, but it's worth a try."

★

Not long after that, Tomi knocked on Helen's door. "I thought I'd take Carl out to play," Tomi said.

Helen frowned, her hands on her hips. "Why would you do that?"

Tomi had thought Helen would be glad to get rid of her brother for a while, and she didn't know what to reply. When in doubt, Roy always joked, tell the truth. Or part of it, Tomi thought. She said, "My friend Ruth, her brother died, and she misses him. Maybe playing with Carl would make her happy."

Helen thought that over. "I guess that's all right." It was cold outside, and Helen told Carl to put on his coat. "He doesn't have mittens. We didn't need them much in San Francisco."

Tomi took Carl's hand in her own mittened hand and led him along the street to Ruth's barracks. Ruth answered the door. She knew what Tomi was up to, of course, and grinned. "Oh, what a cute little boy. Who's he?" she asked.

"This is Carl. His sister Helen takes care of him. They're orphans. I said I'd watch him for a little while. But he doesn't have any mittens, and it's too cold to play outside. Maybe we could read him a story. Do you have any books?"

Before Ruth could answer Carl spotted the pull-toy that had belonged to Ben. "I want to play with the dog," he said.

"Oh no," Ruth told him. She had a horrified look on her face. "Nobody plays with that but Ben—I mean, my mother," she said.

Carl looked disappointed, but he didn't complain. He

took off his coat and sat down on the floor. "You got anything to play with?"

Ruth glanced at her mother, who sat in a chair, looking at the floor instead of at the children. She seemed to be ignoring them.

"I have a pencil. Do you want to draw?" Ruth asked.

Carl nodded, and Ruth gave him a pencil and the back of an envelope.

"Can you draw a horse?" Tomi asked.

"No, a dog. We had a dog. His name was Rusty."

Ruth turned to Tomi, her eyes wide. Then she nodded at the pull-toy. "That's the name of Ben's dog," she whispered.

Carl turned over onto his stomach and began drawing, laughing, and holding up the paper when he was finished. Tomi told him the drawing looked like a fish.

"He's not a fish. He's Rusty." He set the paper back down on the floor and made another drawing. "That's a fish," he said, holding up a picture of a blob. "Let's go outside. I'll draw another animal. I can use a stick in the dirt."

The three put on their coats, and as they left the apartment, Mrs. Hayashi asked quietly, "He's an orphan?"

"He and his brother and Helen. She's only sixteen. She

has to take care of Carl, so she can't work or go to school. She can't even let Carl go outside and play by himself, because he mixes up the barracks and gets lost," Tomi explained.

"Maybe you remember Helen, Mother," Ruth added. "She sang in our church in San Francisco."

They left the apartment, and Carl played outside with Tomi and Ruth until he complained of the cold, and Tomi said it was time to take him home. "I don't think your mom fell for it," she said, disappointed. "She didn't say anything."

"I don't know. Let's go back to the apartment for a few minutes," Ruth told her.

They took Carl back to the Hayashis' barracks. As they walked down the hall, Tomi slipped and knocked against Carl. He giggled and knocked her back on purpose. As they entered the apartment, Carl told Mrs. Hayashi, "She bumped me, but I bumped her good."

Mrs. Hayashi smiled as she rose from her chair. The pull-toy was in her hand. "You may play with this. Very carefully," she said, handing the dog to Carl. Then she nodded at the table. She had covered it with an embroidered white cloth and set of four tiny china cups as thin as butterfly wings on the table. A teapot rested on the table, too. And there was a small bowl of Japanese crackers. Mrs. Hayashi must have brought them from California, because Tomi had not seen them in the camp store.

"Please sit down," Mrs. Hayashi said. When they were all seated, Mrs. Hayashi poured tea into the cups. She was as graceful as a swan Tomi had seen once in California.

"Oh boy, crackers!" Carl said. "Thank you, lady."

"She's Mrs. Hayashi," Tomi corrected.

"You may call me Aunt Hayashi," Ruth's mother said. "And if you are careful, you may play with some other toys I have."

"Wow!" Carl said.

Tomi stared at the table. She was afraid that if she looked at Ruth, Mrs. Hayashi would know they were up to something.

After the tea was finished and Carl was rolling the dog back and forth, Mrs. Hayashi said, "I do not want to keep any girl from school. You may tell your friend I will watch Carl while she attends classes."

"Really? I never thought about that, but I'm sure Helen would be happy. That's a really good idea you have, Mrs. Hayashi," Tomi said. She had to work hard to keep from breaking into a grin.

Mrs. Hayashi cleared away the tea things, and Ruth nudged Tomi in the ribs. "It worked. She thinks it was her own idea," she whispered.

Tomi wasn't so sure, because as she opened the door to leave, Mrs. Hayashi called to her. "Oh, Tomi," she said, and Tomi stopped. "You are a very clever girl."

1943 | CHAPTER TWELVE
ROY *and the* ROYALS

N O W that Helen was back in school, she ought to be happier, Tomi thought. She hoped Helen would smile and crack jokes the way the other bobby-soxers at the camp did. But she was wrong. Helen was as grumpy as ever.

Each morning, Tomi stopped at Helen's apartment to pick up Carl. She took him to Mrs. Hayashi. Then she and Ruth went on to school. Mrs. Hayashi watched Carl until Helen came for him in the early afternoon.

But if Helen hadn't changed, Mrs. Hayashi had. "Now that she spends the day with Carl, Mother's as happy as she can be. She's teaching Carl to fold paper into birds— it's called origami—and they play catch and go for walks. Mother asked your mom to teach her to knit so she can make Carl a pair of mittens."

"I know. Mom told me your mother's even cutting out fabric squares and triangles, and plans to make Carl a quilt," Tomi said.

"She's happy again. She sings all the time. That was a good idea of yours, Tomi."

"Well, Helen isn't happy, and she doesn't sing. She still hates Tallgrass. That's all she talks about. She's in my brother Roy's class, and he told me she's the most bitter person he ever met." He'd also told her Helen was the prettiest girl he'd ever met, as pretty as a pinup. Pinups were the beautiful young women whose pictures were in magazines. Soldiers sometimes tore out the pictures and taped them inside their lockers. Tomi knew her brother had a crush on Helen.

"What's the matter with her?" Ruth asked.

Tomi thought that over as they came across hopscotch squares someone had drawn in the dirt with a stick. She hopscotched to the end of the squares, then hopped around on one foot and went back to the starting point. "I guess it must be hard to have to take care of your brothers when you're only sixteen. Helen blames the government. She told me once she wishes she'd gone to Japan." At the beginning of the war, the government had offered to send any Japanese living in the United States to Japan. A few, mostly those who had been born in Japan and had lived in the U.S. for a short time, left America, but not many.

"Is she *Issei?*" Ruth asked.

"No, her parents were *Issei*. They were born in Japan. She's *Nisei*, second generation." Tomi said. "Helen can't speak Japanese."

"Then why in the world would she want to go to Japan?" Ruth wondered.

"I guess she hates our country that much," said Tomi.

★

One day, Roy announced he and four other high school boys were forming a dance band just like the Jivin' Five band he'd had in California. They would call themselves Roy and the Royals. "*Roy*-als. Get it?" he asked. The band was Roy's idea, and he was in charge. He went to his suitcase where he'd stored his clarinet when the family moved from the house in California, and took it out, playing a few notes. "We've even got our first gig scheduled. Too bad you're little kids or you could come and hear us," he teased Tomi and Hiro.

"I want to go!" Hiro said.

"You can't dance," Roy told him.

"I can dance with Wilson," he retorted. Wilson, Helen's brother, had become his best friend.

"And I can dance with Ruth," Tomi added.

"We will all go," Mom said. "We will go as a family."

"A dance isn't exactly a family event," Roy said.

"We will all go, or none of us will go." Mom gave Roy a stern look. After a year in Tallgrass, many Japanese families in the camp had fallen apart. Families didn't eat with each other, and without real jobs, the men no longer felt they were head of their households. But Mom had done her best to keep the Itanos together. She insisted they go to church together every Sunday and attend the movies with each other. Tomi thought attending Roy's dances was another way to keep the family connection strong.

★

For the next few weeks, Roy and the Royals practiced almost every day after school, in the Itanos' apartment. People in the barracks kept their doors open to listen to the music. Although the walls between the apartments were so thin, they probably couldn't have blocked out the sound if they'd wanted to. Only Helen kept her door closed. Tomi asked her why she didn't want to hear Roy and his friends. Helen said, "It's only noise. I used to dance to a real band at home. I heard Benny Goodman and Tommy Dorsey play," she said, naming two famous dance bands. "And once I went to a Frank Sinatra concert. I heard him sing 'Green Eyes.' He was dreamy. So why would I want to listen to a hick band like your brother's?"

"They're not hicks," Tomi defended Roy. "The guy who plays the saxophone sings sometimes. He's pretty good. I bet if you heard him, you'd think he was Frank Sinatra," Tomi said.

"Bet I wouldn't," Helen replied. "I would know he's not Frank Sinatra because Frank Sinatra isn't Japanese. That means he wouldn't be in this camp. So how could he be singing in your apartment?"

"That's not what I meant," Tomi began.

Helen shut the door in her face. Tomi remembered that word her teacher's husband, the Boy Scout leader, had used—tolerance. It wasn't just white people who didn't have tolerance.

★

Roy and the Royals played their first dance on a Saturday night in the summer of 1943. Tomi wore her red dress, the best of only three dresses she had in the camp. Mom washed Tomi's hair and braided it wet. After her hair dried and Tomi unbraided it, her black hair was a waterfall of curls. Ruth promised to get dressed up, too, just like Mom and Mrs. Hayashi, because Mr. Hayashi promised that after the dance, he would take them all to the canteen. That was what they called the room in the camp where the evacuees bought soda pop and candy bars. It was as close to a restaurant as anything at Tallgrass.

"We're picking up Carl and Wilson on our way," Mom said, then added, "and Helen, of course."

When they reached Helen's apartment, the boys were standing in the doorway waiting, but Helen had on her old dress, and her hair wasn't combed. "I'm not going," she told them.

"Of course, you are," Mom said.

"It's just a crummy little dance. I'd rather stay home."

Mom had had enough. Helen had been bitter and rude ever since she'd moved into the barracks. "My son has a very nice band."

Helen shrugged. "I didn't mean to say—"

"Yes you did," Mom interrupted. "I expect you to come and see for yourself how good it is."

"I'm staying home."

"To do what? Sit in the dark and feel sorry for yourself, the way you always do?"

Mom must have been very angry at Helen, because Tomi had never heard her speak to anyone that way. This must have been another of Mom's changes. Once or twice, she'd even spoken her mind—something that was rare among Japanese women. This was one of those times. "Do you think you're the only one who didn't want to come to this camp? Are you the only one who's been deprived of school and work because you're Japanese? It was Tomi's idea that Mrs. Hayashi would take care of Carl. Have you thanked her?"

Helen stared at Tomi. "I didn't know."

"You don't know how nice people have been to you. Mr. Hayashi is taking us out for a Coca-Cola after the dance, and you would insult him if you didn't come. Now change your dress and brush your hair. We will wait for you." Mom grabbed the door handle and banged the door shut. Then she turned to Tomi and put her hands over face. "Such awful things I said. This place has made me a harsh woman."

Tomi beamed at her. "I bet it worked."

And it had, because in a few minutes, Helen opened the door. She wore a green dress that Tomi had never seen. Not only was her hair combed, but she had put on lipstick.

Mom and Tomi walked behind Helen and her brothers, far enough away so that Mom could whisper. "I am proud of you, Tomi. You don't want to be at Tallgrass any more than Helen does, but you work hard to make the best of it. You try to be happy and to make the people around you happy." Mom took Tomi's hand. "I've seen what you've done for some of the other children to help them adjust to the camp. You are a good girl. And you are a good daughter."

Tomi blushed. She wasn't used to compliments, and she didn't know what to say. She was glad when they reached the Hayashis' barracks and she didn't have to reply. Instead, she admired Ruth's silk dress. Mrs. Hayashi had sewn one of her own dresses to fit Ruth. Mrs. Hayashi was becoming quite a seamstress.

They walked together to the building where the dance was held. Mr. and Mrs. Hayashi led the way, followed by Helen and her brothers. Next came Mom walking alone and finally Tomi and Ruth. As she watched the Hayashis walk arm in arm, Tomi thought how lonely her mother must be without Pop. Mom had written letters asking if Pop could join them at Tallgrass, but nobody had answered her. And Pop's letters didn't say much. He had been transferred to a camp in California, but he didn't tell them why. Tomi wondered if Pop would stay there for the entire war.

The dance floor was lit with colored lights, and high school girls had decorated it with crepe paper streamers. The band was already playing, and couples were dancing. They weren't just high school kids, although the older people left the dance floor when Roy and the Royals played a jitterbug because they didn't understand the new dance steps.

"I wish I could jitterbug," Ruth said, watching the dancers.

"I'll teach you," Tomi replied. "I already know how."

"I'll look silly," Ruth said.

"No you won't. Look at how many other people don't know how to jitterbug, and they're having a good time." Tomi gestured at the couples stumbling around the dance floor. The two girls joined them, and in a minute, they were waving their arms and kicking their heels.

Roy saw Tomi and grinned. He seemed glad his family had come. Tomi noticed him glancing at Helen and realized he was especially glad that Helen had come with them. Tomi and Ruth came close to the bandstand where Roy was. Tomi said, "She's beautiful, isn't she?"

"Who, Ruth?" Roy asked.

"As if you didn't know who I mean! I'm talking about Helen." A boy had approached Helen to dance, but she shook her head. Instead, she stepped out onto the dance floor with Wilson.

"Oh, I hadn't noticed."

"You did so."

Roy blushed, and Tomi knew she was right. "She won't even look at me," he said. "I've tried to start a conversation with her, but she won't say a word."

"Maybe she would if you asked her to sing," Tomi said.

"She sings?" Roy asked.

"She has the most beautiful voice I ever heard," Ruth told him. "She used to sing at church in San Francisco."

Roy shrugged. "We don't play church music. We probably don't play anything she knows."

"You play 'Green Eyes.' I bet she could sing 'Green Eyes,'" Tomi said.

Roy considered that. "You think so?"

"We'll go get her," Tomi said.

She and Ruth made their way across the floor to where Helen and Wilson had just stopped dancing. Helen did indeed look beautiful with her face flushed from the dancing. "You're needed over here," Tomi said. Before Helen could answer, Ruth and Tomi each took one of Helen's hands and all but dragged her to the bandstand. "You know my brother Roy," Tomi said.

"Sure, why?" Helen answered slowly.

"You'll see." She nodded at Roy.

He finished a song. Then as people clapped, he said, "Ladies and Gentlemen, I have a surprise for you. Helen Wakasa, the famous San Francisco songbird, is going to sing 'Green Eyes,' her favorite song."

Helen stared at Roy. Then she turned to Tomi. She didn't look happy. "What is this?"

"You're going to sing," Tomi said. When Helen put her hands on her hips and shook her head no, Tomi added, "You'll look pretty stupid if you don't."

Wilson and Carl ran across the dance floor, grinning at their sister. "Sing, Helen," Wilson said.

"Yeah, sing," Carl said.

"You'll disappoint your brothers if you don't," Tomi told her.

So Helen climbed onto the bandstand, and Roy and the Royals began playing "Green Eyes," Helen's favorite Frank Sinatra song. Helen started out slowly and softly. But as she began to sing, her voice grew louder. She smiled a little. By the time Helen was finished with the song, she was swaying to the music and grinning.

The crowd of dancers loved her, and someone shouted, "More!"

"You know 'Slow Boat to China'?" Roy asked, and without having to be coaxed, Helen nodded. Roy started the music, and Helen sang again. People crowded around the dance stand to hear her. Tomi thought Helen sounded good enough to be in the movies.

As Helen sang "Whatcha Know, Joe?" Tomi moved through the crowd to find Mom. "I bet Roy asks her to join the band," Tomi said.

"And I bet she does just that," Mom replied.

They were right. After that night, Helen became part of the band and sang at every dance. She was a big hit.

Tomi thought singing would make Helen change her attitude, but it didn't. Each morning when Tomi stopped to pick up Carl, Helen would complain about something at the camp. She complained about the apartments and the food and the government.

"I don't get it. Why isn't she happy now?" Tomi asked Mom. Helen had just come into the barracks and slammed her door so hard that Tomi could feel the vibration all the way down the hall.

Mom shrugged. "I don't know. You've done everything you could. Maybe now it's up to Helen."

1943 | CHAPTER THIRTEEN
A CHRISTMAS TREE *for* CARL

T H E week before Christmas, snow fell at Tallgrass. The big flakes covered the ugly barracks and the streets. The snow-covered land looked like Christmas pictures Tomi had seen in magazines. This was her second winter at Tallgrass, and Tomi knew that when the snow stopped, the weather would turn cold and windy. Later, the snow would melt, and the streets would be muddy. But right now, as she stood at the window of the apartment watching the snow come down, she thought the scene was magical.

"It won't be like Christmas at home," Mom sighed. "There won't be a Christmas tree, and I can't bake cookies. We don't have much money for presents. And worst of all, Pop won't be here. Remember how he loved Christmas? It makes me so sad I want to cry."

Tomi was surprised Mom said that, because she usually kept her sadness to herself.

"Maybe he'll be here for Christmas," Tomi said. "Maybe."

Mom shook her head. "Why would the government have sent him to the camp in California if they were going to release him?" Tomi thought she saw tears in Mom's eyes. But Mom smiled and said, "At least Santa Claus will come. Santa won't forget the boys and girls in the camp."

Tomi turned back to the window and watched as Hiro and Wilson ran down the street. Hiro loved the snow, too. Roy had made him a sled from scraps in the workshop. Now, Hiro and Wilson took turns pulling each other on it. Sometimes they took Carl for rides, and Carl clapped his hands with excitement. Carl could play outside, because Mrs. Hayashi had knitted him a cap as well as mittens and bought him a pair of boots.

Hiro and Wilson stopped to make snowballs. They threw them at three girls behind them, and in a minute there was a furious snowball fight. After the boys tired of snowballs, they lay down in the snow and moved their arms and legs to make snow angels.

Then Hiro and Wilson disappeared, and in a minute, they burst through the door of the Itanos' apartment.

"We're going to make a snowman," Hiro said. "How do you make a snowman, Tomi?"

"I don't know," she replied.

"Well, come outside and help us figure it out," Hiro insisted.

"You have to come," Wilson added.

Tomi put on her coat and mittens. The boys ran down the hall ahead of her and out the door. She hurried after them, stepping outside. As Tomi stopped to see where the boys had gone, Hiro yelled, "Bombs away!" and the boys pelted her with snowballs.

"That's a dirty trick," she yelled. But Hiro and Wilson laughed so hard that Tomi couldn't be mad at them. Still, she could get even. Tomi grabbed Hiro and washed his face with snow.

"Hey!" he said. "Why'd you do that?"

"To teach you goofballs not to throw snowballs at me."

Wilson laughed and said, "She got you!"

"And I'll get you, too, if you hit me with another snowball," Tomi said. "Now let's see if we can make a snowman."

"We'll put it by our window so that Carl can see it every morning when he wakes up," Wilson said. "It will make him laugh."

The three of them started with a snowball, then rolled it back and forth in the snow. They patted snow on it until it was a huge snowball. They pushed it in front of the Wakasas' window. They made a second snowball that was a little smaller than the first and placed it on top of the big one. Then they rolled a third ball and tried to lift it on top of the two others, but it fell off. They tried again, but it broke apart.

"We'll just have a short guy snowman," Hiro said.

"Short like Carl," Tomi told him. She went inside and took several pieces of coal from the bucket beside the coal stove. Then she pushed them into the top ball to make eyes and a smile. "We need a carrot for the nose. In pictures of snowmen, they always have carrot noses."

"The only carrots at Tallgrass are cut up and come in cans," Hiro told her. "I know. We can use a pickle."

At noon, Hiro took a pickle from the dining hall and shoved it into his jacket pocket. After lunch, the three returned to the snowman and used the pickle for his nose. "He looks like an old man," Wilson said. "That was a good idea."

"Maybe not so good," Hiro said. "Now my jacket smells like pickles."

"Carl's going to love the snowman. It'll make up a little bit for not having a Christmas tree. We always had one. My mother would put it up when Carl was in bed on Christmas Eve. He'd wake up in the morning, and there it would be, all decorated. We couldn't afford a very big tree, but Carl didn't care. It was having the tree that counted."

★

A few days later, Hiro said, "I wish there was a way we could get a Christmas tree for Carl. He's a little boy. He doesn't understand why Christmas is so different here."

Tomi thought that over. Hiro and Wilson weren't such big boys either. A tree would make them all happy. She thought for a long time. Then she said, "What if we made a Christmas tree?"

"Jeepers! You don't make a tree. They grow," Hiro said.

"I know that. But what if we make a fake tree?"

"Out of what?"

"Roy could get some scraps of lumber from the workshop, and he could build the trunk and branches. Then we could cut out green paper and glue it to the wood for the needles."

"That would be an awful funny-looking tree."

"I didn't say it would look like a *real* tree. But maybe that doesn't matter. After all, Wilson said it was having a tree that mattered."

"How would we decorate it?" Hiro asked.

"We could make paper chains and cut out snowflakes. I bet Mrs. Hayashi would make some origami birds."

"I don't know how we'd sneak it into their apartment."

"We wouldn't. We'd leave it outside their window, just like the snowman." The sun had come out, and the snowman had already melted to half its size.

When Mom and Roy heard Tomi's idea, they were enthusiastic. Roy offered to make a skeleton tree with lots of branches. Mom said she would ask one of the cooks for flour to make flour-and-water paste. Hiro and Tomi could use paper to make paper needles and glue them to the branches.

Each evening, they worked on the tree, cutting out snowflakes and making paper chains and hanging them from the branches. Mrs. Hayashi brought a dozen birds she had made from folding pieces of paper into shapes. Ruth even made a paper star for the top of the tree.

Once Wilson knocked at the door, asking Hiro to come

and play. But Hiro had to say he was sick. He couldn't open the door for fear Wilson would see the tree. It was a surprise for Wilson, too.

The Itanos waited until Christmas morning to set out the tree. They were afraid if they put the tree out earlier, it might snow, and the paper needles and decorations would get wet and fall off. But Christmas morning was clear. Just as the sun came up, they carried the tree outside and placed it directly in front of the Wakasas' window.

"Carl might not see it, so we'll have to tell him it's there," Tomi said.

"Wait until they're awake," Mom told her.

As they passed the Wakasas' door, however, they heard Carl through the thin wall. "Is it Christmas yet, Helen?"

Helen said something the Itanos couldn't make out, and they heard her walk across the floor.

"Can I open my present, Helen?" Carl asked. Wilson had told them that Helen had ordered a sweater from the catalogue for her brother.

"They're awake," Hiro said, and before Mom could stop him, he knocked on the door.

"Merry Christmas," the Itanos shouted when Helen opened the door.

"Not much to be merry about," Helen complained.

"Yes there is," Hiro told her. "Look out the window."

Carl rushed to the window and pushed aside the curtain. Then he turned around, a look of joy on his face. Wilson was behind him. He stared out at the tree, then looked at the Itanos. "A tree? You made a Christmas tree for us?"

Hiro nodded.

"Look, Helen. We have a Christmas tree!" Carl shouted, his face beaming. "It's the best Christmas tree in the camp. Heck, it's the best Christmas tree in the whole world!" Helen slowly went to the window and put her face to the glass. She stared outside for a long time. When she turned around, tears were streaming down her face. "You made a Christmas tree? For Carl?"

"For Carl," Tomi said. "And for Wilson. And for you, too, Helen. We made it for all of you. To make you happy."

The Itanos left then, because they had their own presents to open. Roy closed the Wakasas' door behind them, but seconds later, Helen opened it and called, "Wait."

Tomi had the awful feeling that Helen was going to tell them to take back the tree. She stopped and turned toward Helen.

"Wait up," Helen called, and hurried down the hall to the Itanos. "I just wanted to say ..." She stopped a moment, then smiled. "I just wanted to say Merry Christmas."

1944 | CHAPTER FOURTEEN
THE TALLGRASS SKY QUILT

M O M' S quilting class worked almost every Saturday to complete their first squares. They sewed them together, then made a fabric sandwich of quilt top and back with a batting in between. The batting was fluffy cotton, which would make the quilt warm. The "sandwich" was tacked to an oblong wooden frame that hung from the ceiling of the craft room. The frame was lowered when the women worked on it, then raised to the ceiling for storage.

They were just sitting down around the frame one Saturday in January, 1944, when Mrs. Hayashi rushed in. "I have received the cotton from San Francisco. It came this morning." She untied the package and spread the pieces of fabric over the quilt in the frame. "It is only cotton, not very important," she said. Like other Japanese women, she was modest and did not want the others to think her gift was valuable or that she was bragging. But she beamed as she ran her hands over the beautiful blue material.

"Such lovely fabric," Mom said, picking up a length of material and inspecting it. Even Tomi, who still didn't care about sewing, held her breath as she looked at the beautiful pieces of cloth. Many were a bright indigo blue, but some were faded, others mended. Most were plain, but a few were woven with stripes or plaids. "I believe these were made by hand, not machine," Mom said.

The women took the cloth between their fingers and felt it. They talked about the colors and designs.

"It is only for everyday clothes, mostly for people on farms or in the mountains. Nobody wants such plain stuff," Mrs. Hayashi told them. "Not important," she said again.

"*We* want it," Mom told her. "It will make a beautiful quilt, and because the cloth is heavy, it will be warm. A good thing for this camp."

"Why don't you use the material for the 'tank quilt,' instead of the quilt you just made. Everyone will want to buy a raffle ticket to win such a beautiful quilt," Tomi interrupted.

"A fine idea," a woman said. "The women in Ellis can

make good quilts, maybe better than the one we just finished. But the tank quilt will be different, because women in Ellis have never seen this fabric. Maybe those women will buy our raffle tickets, and we can make even more money for our tank."

Mrs. Hayashi spoke out in her quiet voice. "Are we still hoping to buy a tank? Maybe our money should go to our own young men who are joining the army. They are very brave, and we must support them." Although the government had forced them to relocate, the young Japanese men in the camps were now expected to join the army. They were forming a special unit—the 442nd Infantry. She thought a moment. "I know, we will buy *them* a tank."

"Such a good idea," Mom said. Then she ran her hand over the pieces of blue again, thinking. "This fabric is too thick to be cut into tiny pieces. We must design a special quilt for it."

"We could use a Japanese design," a woman suggested.

"No, it must be an American quilt—American like us," Mom told her, and the women nodded.

The quilters discussed patterns but could not make up their minds. Finally, one said she knew a woman in the camp who was an artist. She would ask her to make a design. The women agreed that was a good idea.

★

The following week, the artist, whose name was Ethel, came to the quilting class. She brought drawings for the quilt. Most American quilts were made up of squares and triangles and rectangles pieced together in a pattern. Ethel's design was abstract, a series of strips of different sizes and shapes. The women smiled when they saw it.

"The design is the sky over the camp late in the afternoon, when it turns so many shades of blue. See, one of the pieces of fabric had a bit of red in it, just the color of sunset." Ethel said. "When it is finished, I will embroider it with lines of silver-white thread, like edges of clouds," Ethel continued. "We will call it 'Tallgrass Sky.' "

"Oh," the women said together, because they knew such thread was expensive and impossible to buy in the camp. Ethel must have brought it with her.

"Such a quilt will be too pretty to put on a bed," someone said.

"Then it will be a wall hanging, a piece of art," Mrs. Hayashi told her. "A very special piece, so we must announce the winner at a very special event."

"A Bon Odori," one of the women said, and the others nodded their agreement. Bon Odori was a festival held in the summer. Women danced in their blue-and-white cotton *yu kata*, as summer kimonos were called, while girls wore colorful silk. Tomi remembered Mom saying once that immigrants brought their traditions with them when they came to the United States, that America was made up of cultures from all over the world. You could still be an American and celebrate Bon Odori.

"But if it is to be a quilt for our American army, shouldn't the winner be announced at an American event?" Mom asked.

"Since it will have red, white, and blue in it, how about Fourth of July?" Tomi blurted out.

"That would be perfect," Mom said. "We will have almost six months until July 4, so there will be time to finish the quilt. And to sell the tickets. The camp newspaper has agreed to print tickets for us. We will each take a few and see if we can sell them."

★

Tomi and Ruth were the best ticket sellers that spring. Each day, they made the rounds of the tables in the mess halls, selling raffle tickets. They sold so many that people held up their hands or shook their heads when they saw the two girls approach. "I already bought one," they'd say.

"I guess we're done," Ruth told Tomi one evening after they had sold only two tickets at supper. "Everybody already has them."

Tomi thought that over. "Everyone in the *camp* has a ticket, but what about the people in Ellis? Remember what the lady said in the quilt class. People in Ellis don't make quilts like ours. I bet we could sell a bunch of tickets in Ellis."

"I don't know. Do you think they would want to win a quilt made by ladies in the camp?"

"Sure, since a ticket costs only a nickel."

Ruth wasn't so confident, but she agreed to go into town with Tomi and find out.

The following Saturday, the two girls got passes and walked out of the Tallgrass gate, past the guards, who waved at them, and down the dirt road to town. They had been to Ellis before. Sometimes they ran errands for their mothers, purchasing things that weren't available in the camp store. At first, people hadn't wanted the Japanese in town. There'd even been "No Japs" signs like the ones Tomi had seen in California. But they were taken down after Ellis residents got to know the evacuees. Some of the Tallgrass men worked on the sugar beet farms. Not many of the townspeople paid attention to the Japanese anymore. But a few still didn't want them around.

Tomi felt self-conscious as she reached Ellis. A woman standing on a porch with her hands on her hips stared at the two girls but didn't say anything. A man drove his car too close to them, and they jumped. He laughed as he drove on. They stopped first at a hardware store, where a girl about their age smiled at them. Then she looked cautiously at the door to a back room. "You can't come in here. I'm sorry," she said in a low voice. "If my father sees you—"

"We're selling raffle tickets for a quilt, only five cents," Tomi said. "It's a beautiful quilt, made by the ladies at Tallgrass."

"You can't stay," the girl whispered.

"Who's out there, Betty Joyce? What are you whispering about?" came a man's voice from the room.

"Two girls. We don't have what they want. They're

leaving," she called, making scooting motions with her hands at Tomi and Ruth.

"But—" Ruth began.

Tomi took her friend's hand and turned around. But she was not fast enough. A mean-looking man came through the doorway. His face turned red and he scowled when he saw the two girls. "Get!" he yelled at them. "We don't allow your kind in here. Where's that sign, Betty Joyce?"

"I'm sorry," Betty Joyce whispered as she followed Tomi and Ruth to the door. She picked up a sign that was lying face down on the floor. The sign said "No Japs" in big black letters. Tomi wondered if Betty Joyce had taken it out of the window on purpose.

"I'd buy a ticket if I had a nickel. I don't hate you," Betty Joyce told Tomi and Ruth, as she put the sign in the window, hiding it behind a display of machine parts.

"It's okay. I don't hate you, either," Tomi told her.

Tomi and Ruth were silent as they walked down the street. Maybe trying to sell tickets in Ellis hadn't been such a good idea. Still, Tomi wasn't ready to give up. When they reached the drugstore, Tomi took a deep breath and looked at Ruth. "Let's go," she said.

"What do you want?" a man behind the counter asked.

He wasn't as mean as the man in the hardware store, but he wasn't friendly, either. Maybe the drugstore had one of those ugly signs, too, Tomi thought.

"We're selling raffle tickets for a beautiful blue quilt the ladies at Tallgrass are making," Tomi said. "They're only five cents."

The man sniffed. "And where's the money going? To help the Japs?"

"It will go to the 442nd Infantry," Ruth told him.

"That's an American division," Tomi added.

"It's made up of Japs," the man said. "Bet you they're a bunch of cowards. You're not selling any tickets in here. Go on with you."

Coming into Ellis had been a mistake, Tomi thought. She bit her lip and took Ruth's hand. But just then, a boy sitting at a table near the soda fountain turned around. "I'll buy a ticket," he said, standing up. He was Dennis, the Boy Scout who had visited Tomi's class the year before. "Hi, Tomi. What kind of quilt are you raffling off?"

"It's all blue with a little red and white. It looks like the sky," she said. "In fact, we call it 'Tallgrass Sky.'"

"I bet I know a few people who would like to win a quilt like that. Why don't you give me some of your tickets, and I'll sell them for you." He turned to a woman nearby and said, "You'd pay five cents to try to win a quilt like that, wouldn't you, Mrs. Stroud? I bet it's as nice as the ones you make."

"Probably better," she said, taking a dime out of her purse and handing it to Tomi. "Some of the boys from Tallgrass are employed on our farm. If the quilters work as hard as those boys do, I know it will be a fine quilt. I'll take two tickets."

"I guess I could buy one," a high school girl told Dennis, counting out five pennies.

By the time Tomi and Ruth left, they had made more than fifty cents, and Dennis had agreed to take the rest of their tickets. He even said he'd ask Mr. Glessner if the Boy Scouts could sell them.

"Don't let that man in there upset you. His son was killed in the South Pacific. He hates everybody," Dennis said.

"I guess I can't blame him. After all, we're Japanese," Tomi said.

"No," Dennis told her. "Like you said once, you're Americans."

1944 | CHAPTER FIFTEEN
POP COMES *to* TALLGRASS

M O M sat in the light from the window, sewing together pieces of the Tallgrass Sky quilt. She didn't even raise her head when there was a knock at the door. "That'll be Wilson. Answer it, Hiro," she said.

"Wilson doesn't knock like that. He always makes three quick knocks," Hiro replied. He was sitting on the floor surrounded by pieces of a paper airplane that he and Roy were putting together.

"Maybe it's Helen," Mom said.

Roy looked up at that. "Nope. Helen's with a friend on the other side of camp, studying for a test," Roy said.

"Then it's Ruth," Mom told them.

"It's not Ruth either. She calls when she knocks," Tomi said. She was sitting on her cot reading a comic book. "But

I'll answer it anyway." There was a second knock, louder this time, as Tomi stood up and went to the door. It must be one of the officials from the camp, she thought. She opened the door slowly and stared at the man standing there. He was dressed in a rumpled suit and scratched shoes. He held a cane in one hand, a fedora hat in the other. The man was stooped and had gray hair. Tomi looked into his face, and for a moment she froze, too surprised to move. Then she cried, "Pop!" She threw her arms around him and said over and over again, "Pop. Pop. Pop." She turned around as if the others hadn't heard her and said, "Pop's come home!"

Mom had already thrown her sewing onto the floor and was rushing to the door. She put her hand on Pop's arm and said, "Sam. You're here. I prayed for this every day." Happy tears fell from her eyes.

Hiro and Roy jumped up from the floor, and now the four surrounded Pop, laughing, hugging, all of them crying, including Pop. "I knew you'd come back," Roy told him.

"Me, too," Hiro said. "Are you going to stay?"

Mom, Roy, and Tomi were quiet as they waited for Pop's answer. Maybe Pop wasn't back at all. Maybe he'd just come for a visit. What if he was being transferred to another camp?

"I'm staying; that is if you let me come inside. I don't want to live in the hall," Pop said.

"Hooray!" Hiro shouted, and they all drew back a little to let Pop enter the room.

They watched as he took a slow step, then another. He used his cane to steady himself. As Tomi stood back to give her father room, she stared at him. Pop had gotten old. He no longer looked like the strong man who could lift crates of strawberries and swing them onto the truck. He had been proud of the way he looked when he dressed up, but now he was shabby. He had lost weight, and his hair was no longer as black as the coal they burned in the stove. He was Pop, but he didn't look like Pop.

Tomi glanced at Mom and saw that she, too, was shocked at Pop's appearance. Mom was frowning.

Roy took his father's arm to lead him to the cot. But Pop shook it off and walked across the room on his own and sat down on a chair. Mom sat next to him and held his hand. "I prayed you'd come home," she said again.

Pop waved away her words, and Mom was quiet.

For a moment, the rest of them were quiet, too, not

knowing what to say. Pop looked around the room, using his cane to push aside the sheet that divided the space in two so that he could see where Roy and Hiro slept. At last, he said to Mom, "You made a little home here. You made a home without me."

"We made a home *for* you," Mom replied.

"Not my home. Where's the kitchen? Do you eat in a mess hall, just like at the prison camp?"

"Oh, it's not so bad. Mom doesn't have to cook. Now she has time to teach sewing," Tomi said.

Pop nodded, but he didn't smile. "So, she has a job instead of being a mother."

Roy shook his head. "It's not like that."

Pop interrupted. "Everything is changed. Everything is different."

"Our family is the same family. And it is complete now that you are home," Mom said. She patted his hand.

"Home," Pop repeated. "I don't want you to say that. A room in a barracks building in a camp that is surrounded by barbed wire will never be a home for me."

"Home is wherever our family is," Mom told him.

"Home is where I say it is." Pop's voice was hard.

Tomi sat down on the floor beside Pop and put her

head against his knee. "Last year, we tried to grow strawberries outside the barracks, but they didn't do very well. You have to show us how, Pop."

He shook his head. "Strawberries don't grow in dirt like this."

"I bet you could make them grow here," Tom said.

"Why should I try?" Pop asked quietly.

Tomi felt like crying—but not happy tears this time. She was confused. Pop had been away for two years. They had hoped every day that he would be released from the prison camp and sent to Tallgrass. But this wasn't the Pop she remembered. This man was old and bitter. What had happened to make him so unhappy?

Maybe Roy wondered about that, too, because he took Pop's arm and said he'd show him around camp.

"I've seen camps like this. Did you forget I've been in prison for the last two years?"

"It's not really a prison camp," Tomi told him. "It's a *relocation* camp. People are staying here until they get jobs. Then they *relocate*. We can get a pass to go into Ellis whenever we want to."

"You think I don't know what a prison is?" Pop replied. "It's a place with barbed wire and guards with guns, where you live in barracks and eat food I wouldn't feed to the pigs back home."

"You are bitter," Mom said. "But you are home ... you are with us," she corrected herself. "Now you must be happy. You have brought us great happiness by coming here."

Pop thought that over. Then he smiled for the first time. "You are right, Sumiko. I have waited a long time to be with my family." He patted Tomi's head and said, "You must tell me how you are doing in school." He turned to Roy. "You are a man now. We must make plans for you." And finally he reached out for Hiro. "My little boy has grown so much I would not have recognized him."

Finally, he squeezed Mom's hand and said, "I missed you. All of you. Now we will be happy that we are together again." He jingled the coins in his pocket. Tomi could hear them clunk against the silver dollar. Pop had kept it all that time.

She squeezed Pop's knee. She was happy, happier than she'd been since the day Pop was taken away. But she was uneasy. Pop was home, but he wasn't the Pop who had left them in California. What had happened to Pop to make him so angry? What if he made the rest of them bitter, too?

1944 | CHAPTER SIXTEEN
POP'S STORY

MOM fixed tea. She put the teakettle on the stove to heat the water, then poured the water on top of the tea leaves in the china teapot. She took out her best teacups, not the everyday cups but the fragile ones that she had packed in California and unwrapped only for tea with Mrs. Hayashi. Other than that, they had been saved for Pop's homecoming.

Although there was a fire in the coal stove, the room was chilly. Pop shivered. Tomi took a blanket off the bed and wrapped it around her father.

He pulled it close and said, "I have been sick, you know."

Roy told him they didn't know. "Too much of what you wrote in your letters was blacked out," he said.

"We don't know anything that happened to you," Mom added. "You must tell us."

"It is over," Pop said. "What good does it do for me to talk about it?" He shrugged.

"Maybe it will help you," Mom said.

Pop scoffed.

"Maybe it will help us, too," Tomi said.

Mom poured the tea into the cups, and holding one with both hands, she gave it to Pop. "Tell us. The truth cannot be worse than what we have imagined."

Pop let the steam rise to his face, then took a sip. He turned to Tomi. "I taught you and your brothers that the two most important things in life were your family and your country. Now I think it is only family."

Tomi felt as if someone had hit her. Was this really Pop talking? He was the most patriotic person she'd ever known. He had taught them America was the best country in the world because it welcomed everyone and gave everyone an opportunity. When Tomi memorized the pledge of allegiance at school, he had given her a dime. He insisted Roy, Hiro, and Tomi speak English at home instead of Japanese, because that was America's language. And at harvest, he donated part of his strawberry crop to a church that gave meals to poor people. He believed he was giving back to the country that had been good to him.

"You don't believe in America anymore, Pop?" Tomi asked.

Pop shrugged. "What kind of country puts people in jail for nothing?" He repeated the word. "Nothing. They charged me with nothing."

"Then why were you in prison for two years?" Roy asked.

Pop finished his tea and handed his cup to Mom. Slowly he began to tell his story.

The FBI men who arrested him took Pop to a jail, where he was held with other Japanese men. The government men sat Pop down at a table and asked him questions. They wanted to know who he was sending information to in Japan. Pop denied he was contacting anyone in Japan except for his parents, who were farmers and very old.

"Then why do you have a radio?" he was asked.

"You can't send messages with a radio. I listen to the baseball games. I like the New York Yankees." When the men didn't smile, Pop added, "Maybe you are not Yankees fans. Maybe you don't even like baseball. Are you un-American?" He smiled, thinking he had made a great joke.

"I ask the questions," one of the men replied.

Then he asked Pop why he had bought so much gasoline and fertilizer. Did he plan to use it to make bombs? The man put his face close to Pop's face.

Pop looked at the man as if he were crazy. "I'm a farmer. I use it on the land. I raise the best strawberries you ever tasted. Come to my house when we are finished here, and my wife will make you a strawberry shortcake. I will give you a nickel if it's not the best strawberry cake you ever ate."

"I've been to your house, and it wasn't for cake."

Pop looked from one man to another. He realized he had better stop joking. This was serious. Mom would be worried if he was late getting home. He wanted the questions to end. Not until that evening did he realize he wasn't going home. He was spending the night in jail.

"Mr. Lawrence got a lawyer for you," Roy said.

Pop shook his head. The FBI men wouldn't let him talk to a lawyer. He never talked to anybody who was on his side.

He was held in jail in California for a few days, not allowed to see anyone. Then he was sent to prison in New Mexico with half a dozen other Japanese men. "They said we were working for the Japanese government, that we were spies. I asked them for proof, and they said they had plenty, but they wouldn't tell me what it was," he said. "I told them I was one-hundred-percent American. They said I wasn't American at all. I wasn't even a citizen."

"But you couldn't be," Roy said. "The law doesn't let Japanese immigrants become citizens. Germans and Italians can, but not Japanese. Only *Nisei*—second-generation Japanese like Hiro and Tomi and me—can be U.S. citizens. How can they blame you for what the law doesn't let you do?"

Pop only shrugged his shoulders.

"They must have believed you finally, because they let you come here," Tomi said.

"They didn't believe me ever. Maybe it's a trick. I think they are watching me all the time, watching you, too."

He shivered again, and Mom put her hand to Pop's forehead to see if he had a fever. "Tell me what is wrong with you. You are not well," she said.

"The camp was very cold, and there were only thin blankets. I didn't have a warm coat. We had to stay outside in the bad weather. I got pneumonia."

Mom gasped. People at Tallgrass got pneumonia from

the cold and the coal smoke that hung over the camp. Some had even died. She said Pop must get into bed. She turned down the blankets on Tomi's cot. Tomi realized that it was Pop's bed now. Mom then told Roy he must find a cot and a blanket for Tomi.

"We will get you well, Sam. You must be well when we go home," Mom told Pop. "The war will be over one day, and we will go back to California and start again. I've been thinking we should raise celery and melons with the strawberries." She smiled at him.

"You tell me what to do? Are you head of the family now?" Pop was angry.

Roy and Tomi exchanged glances. Mom had done everything she could to keep the family together. If Mom hadn't taken charge, who knew what would have happened to them. Pop should be proud of her, not angry.

"It will be your farm," Mom said. "And it won't be long before you are raising the flag over it."

"Bah!" Pop said. "I will never raise the red, white, and blue flag again."

"But you have to, Pop." Tomi didn't like what Pop was saying. "We're Americans. You taught us that."

Pop scowled. "I am not an American."

"You're not Japanese anymore," Mom told him. "The Japanese are our enemy."

"No, I am not Japanese either." Pop stood up and went to the window and looked out over the camp. "What am I? I am nothing."

1944 | CHAPTER SEVENTEEN
A SECOND-CLASS AMERICAN

T H E wind whipped at Tomi's legs as she hurried from her barracks to Ruth's apartment. When she'd first seen snow two winters before, she'd rushed outside and stuck out her tongue to catch the flakes. There had been only snow flurries that day, and Tomi had complained that there'd never be enough snow to make snowballs.

But by now, well into her third winter at Tallgrass, Tomi had seen enough snow to last for a long time—and enough cold. She didn't care if she never saw another snowball. The winter wind whipped across the prairie that day with nothing but barbed-wire fences to stop it. Tumbleweeds pushed by the wind caught on the wire or rolled into the camp and piled up against the buildings. The wind brushed one against Tomi and scratched her hand.

Mom had ordered boots for her from the Montgomery Ward catalogue, and they kept Tomi's feet dry in the slush and mud. But there were the places between the tops of her boots and the bottom of her coat where the wind blew grit from the street onto her bare skin and made it sting with cold. She missed the sunny days in California.

Tomi forgot about California now, as she ran down the street. She thought about what she would tell her friend about Pop. Tomi always went with Ruth to supper. Today, however, she would have to say she couldn't join her friend. Pop had insisted they eat together as a family.

"But it's different here. Families don't sit together in the dining hall," Tomi had protested.

"Our family will sit together," Pop had said in a firm voice. "Our family has broken down since I've been away. I am head of the family now. I say we eat together." He looked at Mom when he said that, and she stared down at her hands, which were folded in her lap. Tomi wondered why Pop blamed Mom for the changes he didn't like.

Tomi realized now that things with the Itanos had changed in many ways since they'd arrived in the camp without Pop. Mom made the decisions, and sometimes she asked Roy and Hiro and Tomi for advice. Before, Pop had made all the decisions and never consulted anybody except Mr. Lawrence. Mom, who rarely left the farm in California, now spent her time working in the camp. She taught the quilting class. She worked with other women making bandages for the war effort and clothes for war orphans. She was even vice president of the Tallgrass Red Cross. She was no longer the shy woman she had once been. Tomi and her brothers had their own lives, too. Without the strawberry fields to work, the three of them had developed new interests. Tomi was proud of them, but Pop wasn't. He wanted everything to go back to the way it was before he was sent to prison.

Well, Tomi was angry, too. She didn't think much of a government that would put her father in jail and make him old and bitter. Maybe America wasn't the country she had believed in. She was confused as she ran down the street to Ruth's barracks.

"Pop's home," she told her friend.

"That's great! You've always said he was fun. I can hardly wait to meet him," Ruth replied.

"He's not so much fun now. He's different. I don't know what's wrong with him, but I don't like it."

"You'll have to find a way to make him happy."

"How can I do that?"

Ruth laughed. "I don't know. You'll figure it out. Come on. Let's go eat."

"That's just it. I can't. Pop says we have to eat together. He wants us to be a family, the way we were in California."

"The fathers were all like that when we came to Tallgrass. But they changed. Mine did. Your father will, too," Ruth told her.

Tomi shook her head. "I don't know. He's pretty stubborn. I'm glad he's here, of course. But I think things will be different from now on."

They already were. They'd changed in the few hours that Pop had been back, Tomi thought as she returned to the Itanos' apartment. She was different, too. Pop's treatment had made her think about things she had always taken for granted. She glanced up at the American flag that was whipping back and forth in the wind. The flag always made her proud. Pop had taught her to put her hand over heart when she passed it. Sometimes, she even saluted it. But now, she walked on past it, her hands at her sides. After the way Pop had been treated, maybe that flag didn't mean so much.

Pop frowned at Tomi when she returned. He was not

pleased she had taken so much time. "You must not keep me waiting," he said.

"But I had to tell Ruth I couldn't eat with her. That would have been rude," Tomi protested.

"She should understand your family is more important."

"Yes, sir."

"And Sumiko." Pop turned to Mom. "I don't like you wearing pants. You must put on a dress." Like many of the women at the camp, Mom wore slacks almost every day. They were not only more comfortable than dresses, but they protected her legs from the wind and dirt.

Tomi exchanged glances with Roy and Hiro as they followed Mom and Pop out of the apartment. "He'll be okay," Roy whispered. "He just has to make sure we know he's the boss. Once Pop finds a job here, Mom can stop working, and that'll make him happy."

"Maybe she likes to work. Why should she have to stop?" Tomi asked.

"Yeah, there's nothing for her to do in the apartment except stare out the window," Hiro said.

"She's a Japanese woman. She should do what her husband says. That's what Pop thinks." Roy told them.

"I thought she was an American." Hiro seemed confused.

"Maybe not," Tomi said. "Maybe we're not Americans either."

★

The dining room was crowded, and the Itanos had to wait until people finished eating to find five places together. Pop complained about the food. It was no better than what he had eaten in the prison camp. He scowled at the noise and the children running around. There were no manners at Tallgrass, he said.

"But we are together, Sam," Mom told him. "Everything will be all right now."

Pop patted her hand and smiled. He hadn't smiled much since he'd arrived.

As they finished eating, Mrs. Glessner, Tomi's teacher, stopped at the table and held out her hand. "Are you Mr. Itano? I know Tomi must be very happy you are here."

Pop only frowned at her hand and didn't take it. "She would be happier if we were at home in California," he said.

"Sam!" Mom exclaimed at Pop's rudeness.

Mrs. Glessner wasn't offended. "We would all be happier if there were no relocation camps," she said. She smiled at Pop. "Tomi is one of our best students. You should be proud of her. She wrote a beautiful essay about the flag in the camp. It was the best in the class."

"Bah," Pop said. "I know what that flag means for us. It means living behind a barbed-wire fence."

Mrs. Glessner nodded. "You are very angry. You have a right to be. But I hope you will not turn your children against their country. And I hope you will read Tomi's essay."

Tomi looked down at her plate. She did not want Pop to read the essay. She didn't feel so great about what she'd written. When she got back to the apartment, she would put it into the stove. Maybe she didn't believe what she had written anymore.

★

"Will Pop always be this way?" Tomi asked Mom several weeks later. Pop had criticized Tomi that morning for acting foolish.

"We can't goof off anymore," she'd told Hiro.

Mom shook her head at Tomi's question. "I don't know." She had a worried look on her face. "*Shikata ga nai*."

Mom was right. It couldn't be helped. Tomi had tried. She had shown Pop around the camp. She'd taken him to the print shop where evacuees made posters about winning the war. They'd gone to Hiro's baseball game. Tomi had introduced Pop to men who were building a Japanese garden out of sand and rocks and plants outside the barracks. But Pop hadn't paid much attention. Now, he was outside with two other men, both complainers, talking about the government. They squatted down under the window, and Tomi could hear their voices grow louder as they talked about their treatment at Tallgrass.

Maybe they were right, Tomi thought. She'd complained to Ruth about the fence and the food the day before, and Ruth had told her she sounded just like Pop. "Maybe he knows what he's talking about," she had responded.

"Tomi!" Ruth replied. "That doesn't sound like you. You always look at the good side of things."

"Maybe there isn't a good side anymore," Tomi said.

The two girls were watching a high school baseball game that day. The Tallgrass team was playing against a team from Ellis High School. People in the camp loved baseball, and they were crowded around the field watching the game. The Ellis farm boys were better at bat, but the Tallgrass players outshone them as fielders.

The game was a close one. In the bottom of the ninth inning, Ellis was leading by only one run. Roy was one of the best hitters, and Tomi clutched Ruth's arm when he came up to bat. "Now we'll win," she said.

Roy swung at the first pitch and hit a foul ball. He let the next pitch go by, and the umpire called it a ball. Roy swung and missed on the third pitch. Then he hunkered down, and Tomi thought this time, Roy would hit the ball so hard it would go over the barbed-wire fence. As the pitch came, Roy moved back a little and didn't swing. "Strike three, you're out!" the umpire called. Roy dropped his head and walked away from home plate.

The umpire was wrong. It wasn't fair, Tomi thought. And suddenly, she raised her fist and yelled, "The umpire's a lunkhead!" Tomi had never said anything like that before, and Ruth stared at her with a surprised look on her face. Others turned to stare at Tomi, too. Japanese girls didn't yell at umpires.

Tomi realized what she'd done. She glanced at a

woman who frowned at her. "Well, he is a lunkhead," Tomi said in a loud voice. "He made that call because Roy's Japanese. If Roy'd been a white boy, that pitch wouldn't have been a strike."

Ruth grabbed the sash of Tomi's dress and pulled her back. "Be quiet. People are looking at you," she said.

"So what? Maybe I'm tired of being a second-class citizen."

1944 | CHAPTER EIGHTEEN
POP *and the* ROYALS

A FEW weeks after Pop arrived in Tallgrass, Tomi persuaded him to attend a dance where Roy and the Royals were playing. Of course, Pop had listened to the band practice in the Itanos' apartment, but he'd never heard them perform in public. So now, Pop sat with Mom, Hiro, and Tomi at a table in the big building where the dances were held, sipping a Coca-Cola that Roy had bought him.

Pop tapped his foot to the music. Then he said, "You want to dance, Sumiko?" He took Mom's arm, and in a minute, they were dancing a slow dance called a fox trot.

"I didn't know they could dance," Hiro said, grinning at Tomi.

"Me neither." She smiled, too, but the one who was

smiling the most was Roy. He was playing his best that night, and Tomi knew that was because Pop was there. Roy wanted Pop to be proud of him.

The Royals played another slow dance, and Mom and Pop stayed on the dance floor. When the band switched to a jitterbug, the two of them returned to the table. That new dance was too confusing for him, Pop said. It wasn't confusing for Hiro and Tomi, however, and they rushed out onto the dance floor and began jerking around. They weren't very good, Tomi knew, but that didn't matter. Pop clapped in time to the music and grinned at them. Then the band played, "Whatcha Know, Joe?" and chanted the words: "Whatcha know, Joe? I don't know nothin'."

When that song was over, the Royals played another slow tune, and Pop stood up and bowed to Tomi, took her hand, and led her to the dance floor. Then Hiro stood and bowed to Mom in exactly the same way, and in a minute, they, too, were dancing.

It was the best time Tomi had had since she came to Tallgrass, certainly the best time since Pop had joined them. She hoped Pop was feeling better about the camp.

When the dance ended, the four sat down at the table again and listened to Helen sing. "She has a very pretty voice," Pop said. "But I wish she would sing a Japanese song."

Tomi was afraid Pop would criticize America again, but he only sat, beating time to the music, his fingers tapping the table.

When the band took a break, Roy came over to them. "What do you think of the Royals, Pop?" he asked.

"Pretty good," Pop said. "But why don't you play some Japanese music?"

"Japanese?" Roy asked. "Heck, Pop, you can't dance to Japanese music."

"There is Japanese dancing."

"Not on a dance floor in the good old U.S. of A." Roy picked up Tomi's Coca-Cola and took a sip. "Look at all these people. They're here because they like American dancing."

Helen came to the table, and nodded at Mom and Pop. When she'd first met Pop, she'd held out her hand, but Pop had stared at it instead of shaking it. Now she didn't offer to shake hands. "You like it any better at Tallgrass?" she asked.

"I would like it better if we were home in California," he replied.

"Me, too, but it won't be long now. We're winning this war. We'll win it even faster if Roy joins up."

Roy nudged her with his elbow to be quiet. "Right now, I've got to get back to work," he said. He started for the bandstand, then stopped and turned around. "I've got a surprise for you, Pop." He whispered something to Helen as they started across the dance floor. She nodded.

Roy picked up his clarinet and blew a few notes. People returned to the dance floor and waited for the music to begin. Instead of launching into a tune, however, Roy said in a loud voice, "Folks, may I have your attention?"

People stopped talking and turned to him. "We have a very special guest here tonight. My pop. He hasn't been at Tallgrass very long, and this is his first dance. So I'm going to play his favorite song for him. He taught it to me when I was little. It's not really a dance tune, but I think you know it."

People clapped and turned to our table. Pop rose and bowed to them, very happy.

"Ready, Helen?" Roy asked. She nodded. "Okay, Pop, here it is." He whispered something to the band. Then he played a few notes on his clarinet.

Pop beamed at him and said, "Now a real Japanese

song." But it wasn't a Japanese song. Instead, the Royals launched into "America."

As the dancers recognized the music, they began to sing, "My country 'tis of thee ..." Some of them turned to Pop and nodded their approval.

Pop recognized the song, too. The smile faded from his face. He turned his back to the band and scowled. "Bah! That's not my favorite song anymore," he said. Then he stood up and said, "Come on, Sumiko. We're going home."

"We can't leave now. You'll hurt Roy's feelings," Mom protested.

"I don't care. Roy should know better and so should you." Pop started toward the door, his cane banging on the floor. Mom gestured at Hiro and me to follow.

"What's wrong with him?" a girl asked Tomi.

She started to explain that Pop had been in a prison camp where he was badly treated. But she didn't. Pop had a right to be angry. So she said, "Nothing's wrong with him. It's what's wrong with this country," Tomi told her.

★

After that, Roy and the Royals didn't practice in the

Itanos' apartment anymore. In fact, Roy stayed away from Pop as much as he could. He even started eating meals with his friends again. "I honor Pop, but I don't agree with him. I want to be a good son and don't want to be disrespectful. So it's better I keep out of his way," Roy told Tomi.

"Well, I do agree with him. He's gotten rotten treatment, and he has a right to dislike America," Tomi said.

"I wish you didn't feel that way, especially since I'm going to tell you a secret," Roy said in a serious way.

Tomi looked up, waiting.

"As soon as I turn eighteen, I'm going to join the army," Roy said.

Tomi's mouth dropped open. "Do you have to?"

"If I don't, I might get sent to a prison camp like Pop," he explained.

Tomi knew that the young men in the camp were being asked to join the army—the all-Japanese 442nd, which was known as the "Go for Broke" unit. Everyone in camp was proud of the 442nd, because the soldiers were so brave. Still, some of the men refused to join. They asked why they should fight for America when the country put their families into the relocation camps. There had been arguments and even fistfights at Tallgrass over enlistment.

Tomi knew that sooner or later, Roy would have to make a decision about joining the army, so his secret shouldn't have surprised her. Still, she hoped the war would be over by the time he turned eighteen that summer.

"Maybe you could just get a job in the camp to help the war effort so you won't have to join up," Tomi said.

"You don't understand. I want to join. I want to fight for my country."

"Why? Why, after the way America treated Pop? We hardly recognized him when he came here. He left California a strong man, and now he walks with a cane. He used to be so happy, but he never smiles anymore. Look what America did to him."

"You're right about Pop, but I still love this country. You do, too."

"I'm not so sure anymore, not after the way Pop was treated," Tomi told him.

"Don't say that," Roy said quickly.

"It's true," Tomi said. "I'm sorry I sold raffle tickets to help the war effort. And I think you're dumb to join the army."

"You shouldn't say all that," Roy told her.

"*Shikata ga nai*," said Tomi. "It can't be helped."

★

On the day he turned eighteen, Roy told Pop he was going into the army.

"No!" Pop exclaimed. "No son of mine is risking his life to fight for America. You do not have my permission. I forbid it!" He hit the floor so hard with his cane that it left a dent in the wood.

"It's too late, Pop. I already signed up."

"I did not agree."

"You don't have to," Roy said. "I'm eighteen. I can sign up on my own."

"You go against my wishes?"

Roy sighed. "Look, Pop. There isn't much choice. I can sign up, or I can refuse. And if I refuse, I'll be arrested. Then I'd have to go to prison like you did."

"At least it would be for a reason. I was there just because I am Japanese."

"Come on, Pop."

Pop put up his hand. "Look at your mother. She is crying. Did you think of her?"

Roy looked miserable, and Tomi wondered if he was

sorry now that he had enlisted. "I can't help it. It's too late."

Pop stood and hobbled to the window. "This is what this country has done to us. It has split our family apart. And now you want to fight for it?" Pop shook his head and stared out the window.

Tomi came up beside Pop and took his hand, and when she looked into his face, she saw tears.

She didn't hate America the way Pop did, but she didn't like it very much.

1944 | CHAPTER NINETEEN
ROY JOINS *the* ARMY

THE family saw Roy off at the Tallgrass gate. He grinned and waved. The Itanos waved back, even Pop, but he looked grim. Only Mom smiled, as she handed Roy a paper sack with his lunch in it. She had asked one of the cooks to make Roy's favorite Japanese food for the bus ride.

"Where's Hiro?" Roy asked, as the young men started to board the bus. He looked around at the people gathered at the gate. Hiro had been with them, but he'd disappeared. Tomi craned her neck to see over the crowd, and then she spotted Hiro running from the barracks. "Gangway," he yelled as he pushed through the crowd. He rushed up to Roy and said, "I almost forgot. Hold out your hand." When Roy did, Hiro dropped something into it.

"Your flag pin!" Roy said. Hiro had won the red, white,

and blue flag pin in the paper drive at school.

"It's my favorite thing. It will keep you safe," Hiro said.

For a moment, Tomi thought Roy would cry, but he didn't. Instead, he attached the pin to his shirt and said, "Thanks, soldier." He saluted Hiro. Hiro saluted back, then grinned and said, "Whatcha know, Joe?"

Pop didn't say anything against the army then or even about the flag. He just stared as Roy climbed aboard the bus with the other enlistees.

The bus started up, then pulled out of the gate. A guard shut the gate, and people went back to the barracks, but not the Itanos. They stayed until the bus disappeared, stayed until the dust settled back onto the dirt road.

★

Tomi lagged behind her family as they walked back to their apartment. She kicked at the dirt with the toe of her shoe. The wind came up. It seemed the wind always blew at Tallgrass. Tomi rubbed her eye to get out a piece of grit that had blown into it. She wished she were back in California, walking through the strawberry fields, the early-morning light shining on the green leaves, the mud squishing up through her bare toes. At Tallgrass, the light was harsh and made her squint.

Ruth was outside her barracks waiting when Tomi walked by. "You want to play?"

"Play what?" Tomi asked.

Ruth shrugged. There wasn't much to do at Tallgrass. They could play hopscotch or jacks, but Tomi was tired of those games. "I wish we had a swimming pool," Ruth said.

"Yeah, why would the government build us a pool? We're just Japanese internees. Who cares about us?" Tomi asked.

"You've been in a bad mood ever since your dad came here," Ruth said.

"Wouldn't you be if your father had been treated the way mine was?"

Ruth shrugged. "The war's going to be over before long. You should look ahead."

"At what?"

"You're no fun, Tomi. Maybe I'll play with somebody else."

"Go ahead," Tomi told her.

Ruth turned to go, then stopped. "I know why you're upset. It's about your brother joining the army, isn't it?

I'm sorry, but I bet he turns out to be a real hero." When Tomi didn't respond, Ruth added, "I'll miss the dances. Nobody's as good as Roy and the Royals."

At that, Tomi smiled a little. "Come on, let's get a pass and go into Ellis. Roy gave me a dime. I'll treat you to an ice-cream cone."

★

The drugstore was crowded when the two girls walked in, and they had to wait in line. As Tomi was making up her mind whether to order chocolate, strawberry, or vanilla ice cream, Dennis came up to her.

"I was afraid I'd have to go all the way out to Tallgrass to give you this money," Dennis said, digging into his pocket and taking out two dollar bills and several coins along with a handful of ticket stubs with names written on them. "I sold all the raffle tickets you gave me. The word's out that the ladies at Tallgrass are real good sewers. Everybody wants a chance to win the quilt." He turned to another boy. "They're selling tickets on a quilt to raise money for the war effort."

"Which side is it going to?" the boy asked and snickered.

"Hey, that's not nice," Dennis told him, glancing at Tomi. In the past, Tomi would have put the boy in his place, but now she didn't care. When Tomi failed to reply, Dennis asked the boy, "Haven't you heard of the 442nd infantry? They're the bravest soldiers out there, and a lot of them came out of Tallgrass."

"Can't you take a joke?" the boy asked. He turned to Tomi. "I didn't mean anything by it."

"Who cares?" Tomi replied.

Dennis said, "I bet I can sell more tickets if you have them. I ran out."

Tomi shook her head. "I'm not selling tickets anymore. Why should I try to raise money for the war effort when the government treats us like we're the enemy?" She took the money and the ticket stubs from Dennis and put them into her pocket. "I'll give all this to Mom, but I'm not bringing you any more tickets."

1944 | CHAPTER TWENTY
RUTH PICKS *the* WINNERS

FOURTH of July was a big day at Tallgrass. In fact, it wasn't much different from the celebrations in Ellis or back in California. Children decorated bike and wagons wheels with red, white, and blue crepe paper in the spokes. Grown-ups waved American flags or attached them to their hats. They wore red, white, and blue shirts and dresses. A few women put on their blue-and-white kimonos, because the Fourth of July was a special occasion.

A marching band made up of musicians at Tallgrass had been practicing patriotic songs for weeks. The boy who had ranked highest in the high school graduating class carried the American flag. The highest-ranking girl held the Colorado flag.

The parade began at noon. The two flag bearers led it.

Next came the band playing "The Star-Spangled Banner." Men who were lined up along the street took off their hats when they heard the national anthem. People put their hands over their hearts as the flag passed. Behind the band was a truck of Japanese boys who were leaving for the army the next day. Children pulled the wagons they had decorated, some with small kids riding in them. Then came the camp's Boy Scouts and Girl Scouts, and to everyone's surprise, there were scouts from Ellis marching with them. Among them was Dennis as well as Betty Joyce. She was the girl from the hardware store whose father had been so mean when Tomi sold raffle tickets.

Farmers pulled wagons displaying the vegetables they had grown at Tallgrass. One man had set up a Japanese garden in a cart. Everyone clapped as the floats went by, but they clapped hardest for two Tallgrass soldiers who had been wounded and then discharged. They were riding in a car, and boys ran beside them and saluted.

Everyone agreed it was the finest parade they had ever seen. When it was over, they crowded around the tables for lunch. Then a master of ceremonies called for attention. He was standing on a wooden stage made for the event. It had stairs on both sides of it. He announced the winners of the best float and of the flower-arranging contest. Then came the drawing for the Tallgrass Sky quilt.

Mom and Mrs. Hayashi had hung the quilt from a pole at the back of the stage. It was even more beautiful than Tomi had expected. There were long strips of blue with a tiny piece of red hidden among them. The silver thread shone in the sun like diamonds. Tomi had never seen anything like it. Still, she wished the women had not made a red, white, and blue quilt. It was too American.

Mom stood on the platform beside the quilt, because she was in charge of the raffle. The master of ceremonies introduced her and asked her to tell about the quilt. Tomi hadn't wanted to come to the Fourth of July celebration at all, but Mom had insisted the whole family attend. She said they would dishonor Roy if they stayed away. So Tomi stood beside Pop, who scowled. He didn't like Mom standing up there talking to all those people.

Mom didn't pay any attention to him, however. She came forward and told how the women had learned to quilt in a class at Tallgrass. They had never quilted before, she said, but they learned quickly. She gave the names of the women who made the quilt, and people clapped. "Now it's time to draw the name of the winner," she said, and looked around until she spotted Tomi. "I think we should ask the girl who sold the most raffle tickets to draw."

Tomi shrank back as Mom beckoned to her. She didn't want anything to do with the quilt now.

"Come on, Tomi," Mom said, but Tomi stepped behind Pop. Then Pop looked at Mom and shook his head no. "I guess she's shy," Mom said, looking around. She spotted Ruth and said, "Ruth Hayashi, will you draw the winner?"

Ruth was shy, too, but still, she stepped onto the stage. Mom picked up a big glass jar of ticket stubs and swirled them around with her hand. "Now, Ruth, you pick the winner," she said.

Ruth reached into the jar and pulled out a ticket, holding it at arm's length. Then she grinned at the crowd and said, "Sorry, I picked my own name." She dropped the stub back in the bowl. The crowd laughed, but Tomi didn't. She wished Ruth, too, had refused to pick the ticket. But Ruth's father hadn't been sent away to a prison camp. She didn't feel the way Tomi did.

"Okay, this one," Ruth said, choosing another ticket and handing it to Mom.

Mom took the ticket and squinted at it. Then she said, "The winner of the Tallgrass Sky quilt is Rose Iwasaki."

A woman in the crowd gasped and put her hands over her face. People began to move away, but Mom called, "Wait a minute. We have a surprise. We raised so much money that we are giving away another quilt. It is the first quilt we made."

Tomi felt jealous when Mom and Ruth grinned at each other.

"Okay," Ruth said. She held her hand over the jar for a long time. Then she snatched up a ticket and gave it to Mom.

Mom read it and frowned. "Oh, American names are so hard to read," she said.

Everyone laughed, except for Pop and Tomi. In fact, Pop looked annoyed that Mom was having such a good time entertaining people. Tomi thought that later Pop might tell Mom that Japanese women were supposed to be shy and quiet, the way Mom used to be. Since she'd arrived at Tallgrass, she'd become outgoing and enjoyed entertaining people.

"The winner is Mary Stroud," Mom said.

"She has the farm across the road," a woman behind Tomi whispered. "Her husband was the first one to give jobs to boys from the camp. I'm glad she won."

People moved away from the platform and went back to the tables for dessert. After that, the townspeople began to leave. As Tomi passed one of the Girl Scouts, the girl said, "You Japs sure know how to throw a party."

"We *what?*" Tomi asked.

"You Japs." The girl thought that over. "Sorry. I guess you say Japanese."

Tomi didn't reply. Instead, she stuck out her tongue at the girl.

1944 | CHAPTER TWENTY-ONE

WHAT'S WRONG *with* TOMI?

"I'M disappointed with Tomi," Mrs. Glessner told Mom and Pop not long after school started in the fall. Tomi was in the ninth grade; Mrs. Glessner was her teacher again. She had come to the Itanos' apartment one afternoon to talk about Tomi's behavior.

Pop frowned as he glanced at Tomi. She was sitting on the bed, staring at the floor. "Is she a bad girl at school?" Pop asked.

"No, nothing like that. Tomi has always been polite. She is a nice girl."

"Then what is the matter?" Mom asked. She had fixed tea, and now she handed one of the special cups to Mrs. Glessner, who took it with both hands.

Mrs. Glessner took a sip. "Such good tea," she said.

"That's because my wife uses real tea, loose tea, not American tea bags," Pop told her. "And no sugar and milk in it, like you Americans."

"Sam," Mom said, putting her hand on his arm.

Pop shook it off. "I will say what I want in my own apartment," he told her.

"I understand, Mr. Itano," Mrs. Glessner said. "Relocation has been hard on you. It has been hard on everyone. And I know it is hard on Tomi." She glanced at Tomi, who still didn't look up.

"I thought she had adjusted to Tallgrass," Mrs. Glessner continued. "She was doing so well with her schoolwork. She was my best student."

"And now?" Mom asked.

Mrs. Glessner took another sip of tea. "Now, she doesn't turn in her homework. She doesn't participate in class discussion. Tomi doesn't care about school anymore. I think something is wrong."

Mom glanced at Tomi, then shrugged.

"Maybe she is worried about her brother in the army," Mrs. Glessner suggested.

"What's wrong is she is locked up in this camp," Pop said, anger in his voice. "Wouldn't you be upset if you

were treated like a criminal? What would you do if someone took away your home and made your family live in one
room? Look at this ugly building and those dirt streets.
This isn't home. This is a jail. And you expect Tomi to be
happy? And work hard at school? For what?" Pop slammed
down his cup so hard that it shattered.

"Oh!" Mom said. The cups had been a wedding present
and were her most precious possession.

Pop looked down at the broken pieces but didn't say
anything. Instead, he reached for his cane and left the
room. They could hear his cane tapping as he walked down
the hall and went outside.

"I'm so sorry," Mrs. Glessner said, picking up the
broken pieces of porcelain. "Such a lovely cup. Can it be
mended?"

"Do not concern yourself," Mom replied. "I am more
worried about whether Tomi can be mended."

"I'm not broken," Tomi spoke up for the first time.
"Pop's right. Why should I care about school? All I'm ever
going to be is an internee."

"The war will be over, and then you'll have lots of
opportunities," Mrs. Glessner told her.

"Sure," Tomi said. "Even if we leave the camp, what

will happen to us? People will hate us. They'll still call us Japs. We won't ever be able to return to California."

"You don't know that, Tomi," Mom said.

"Do you think Mr. Lawrence will let us go back to our farm?" Tomi asked.

"He promised we could," Mom said.

"He hasn't even written you a letter. Martha hasn't written me either. I bet she threw away Janice." Janice was the Japanese doll Tomi had left with Martha for safekeeping.

"They don't know where we are. How could they write?" Mom asked.

"They don't care. Nobody cares about us. Why should I care about us either?"

Mrs. Glessner set her cup carefully on the table and stood up. "I am sorry you feel that way, Tomi. You are a bright and clever girl. I have been told it is the Japanese way to look ahead with hope, not to look back with anger. But perhaps I am wrong."

"No," Mom replied. "You are not wrong."

★

After Mrs. Glessner left, Tomi said she was going outside.

"No, you will stay and talk to me," Mom said.

Tomi sighed and curled up on the cot with her back to Mom.

"You will sit up and look at me. I miss my happy little girl who was so helpful," Mom said.

Tomi sat up and stared at Mom, a stern look on her face. "You're going to tell me I have to do better in school. Well, I don't care about school, and that's that."

"You are so angry now. Is it because of Pop?"

Tomi shrugged. Mom already knew the answer.

"He has changed a great deal, and I worry about him. I wish you would help him. Instead, you support his anger. You make it worse," Mom said.

Tomi shrugged and didn't answer.

Mom stared at Tomi for a long time. "Now you may go," she said in a sad voice. "Go play with Ruth."

"Ruth doesn't like to play with me much anymore," Tomi said.

"You are not much fun to be around. Do you blame her?" Mom asked.

★

Two weeks later, when Pop was out, Mom took a letter from under a pillow and gave it to Tomi. "This came for you. I hid it because it's addressed to you, and I didn't want anyone else to open it," she said. Pop believed he had the right to open any mail that was sent to a member of the Itano family. Tomi had never received a letter. "I think it's from Roy," Mom added. Roy wrote every week, but the letters were always addressed to the family.

Tomi snatched the letter and tore it open. "It *is* from Roy!" she said. "He wrote a letter just to me. Should I read it out loud?"

Mom smiled. "If you want to."

Tomi sat down on a chair and held the letter in front of her.

Dear Tomi, she began. She liked the idea that Roy had written just to her, and she read the beginning again, *Dear Tomi*.

She continued.

This letter is just between you and me, because I need your help. We all need your help.

Tomi looked up at Mom and frowned, then returned to the letter.

I am worried about Pop and what he is doing to our family. Since you are the favorite child, I think you are the only one who can help him.

"I'm the favorite?" Tomi asked.

Mom shrugged. "There is no favorite. But if there were ..." She smiled.

What I'm asking you to do will not be easy.

Tomi stopped and began to read to herself.

"Well, what does he say?" Mom asked.

"It's my letter."

Mom nodded.

Tomi read silently.

I worry about you, too. You never let anything get you down before. You were the one who kept our spirits up. You helped everybody adjust to Tallgrass. Remember Carl's Christmas tree and how it made all the difference for Helen? That was your idea. But after Pop came home, he made you unhappy. You changed, and that made the rest of us unhappy.

Tomi stopped and took a breath.

I think you are the only one who can help Pop. I don't know how, but you have to think of a way or our family will never be the same.

I know you are angry at America. I am, too, sometimes. But it is our country, and we have to do what is best for it and for our family. That's why I joined the army. I had to fight for America. I thought Pop would be proud of me for doing that, but it didn't work.

One day the war will be over, and Pop will have to find work. What will happen to him with his attitude? Who would give him a job? Would Mr. Lawrence hire someone so angry? What would happen to Mom and you and Hiro?

I think you know it is the Japanese way not to look back with anger but to look ahead with hope. Mom has tried to help Pop. Hiro is too young. I upset Pop. So you see, Tomi, it is up to you.

Your brother

Roy

Tomi stared at the letter for a long time. Then she looked up at Mom. "That last part about anger and hope ... you told him to write to me, didn't you?"

Mom nodded. "Sometimes I write to him on my own. You won't tell Pop, will you? I am so worried about him."

"And me?" Tomi wondered.

"And you, too," Mom admitted. "I worry about you."

"Am I as unhappy as Pop?" Tomi asked.

Mom shook her head. "'No, but I am afraid you will be one day. You are so young. I did not want you to spoil your life with hatred."

Tomi handed the letter to Mom, who read it to herself, then folded it and put it back inside the envelope, telling Tomi to keep it in a safe place. They wouldn't want Pop to read it.

"What do I do, Mom?" Tomi asked. "I can't change Pop."

"Maybe you can. I hope you will think of a way."

1945 | CHAPTER TWENTY-TWO
THE CONTEST

"COME on, Pop. Come build a snowman with Hiro and me," Tomi pleaded.

Pop sat in his chair in the apartment, a blanket around his shoulders. "Bah! I don't like this snow. It makes me ache all over. We never had snow in California. Why would I go outside and make a man out of snow?" He pulled the blanket closer.

"It's fun," Hiro told him. "And after a while, you won't feel the cold."

Pop waved them away, and Tomi and Hiro went outdoors by themselves.

"He isn't any fun anymore, is he, Tomi?" Hiro asked. "He never jokes or plays with us. Remember when it was hot outside on the farm in California? Pop would turn on the hose and let us run through the water to cool off?"

"We wouldn't want to run through it today," Tomi told him.

"I like the cold. After we build the snowman, Wilson and I are going ice skating." The fire hydrant had been opened to flood the ball field, turning it into a skating rink. Last year, before he left for the army, Roy had made ice skates for the two boys. He made them out of pieces of metal, with straps they could use to tie the skates to their shoes. Hiro added, "I like Tallgrass. We couldn't go ice skating in California. This is a good place."

Tomi studied her brother for a moment. Tallgrass was a real home for Hiro and Wilson. They had a baseball field and an ice rink. They explored the prairie around Tallgrass for snakeskins and arrowheads. And they made kites to fly in the brisk Colorado wind. The children had adjusted to the barracks and harsh land and to the change of seasons. It was the older people such as Pop who still resented the camp.

Tomi wished she could find a way to help Pop. Mom and Roy were counting on her, but nothing had worked. She'd tried to get Pop to play with Hiro and her, but Pop wouldn't do it. She'd invited him to school programs and plays and concerts, but he wouldn't go. He sat in the apartment all day, grumbling. Tomi had just about given up.

Wilson joined them, and Tomi helped the two boys make two snowballs for the snowman. Then she stacked one on top of the other. "Let's make him a soldier," Hiro suggested. "Come on. I bet Helen would make a cap for him. And we can find a piece of wood for his gun."

The two boys saluted the snowman, and Hiro said, "Whatcha know, Joe?" Then they took off, leaving Tomi alone.

Mom was teaching her quilt class, and Tomi didn't want to return to the apartment. Pop was there, and she didn't care to listen to him complain. She thought she might go to the library, but just then, Mrs. Glessner came up to her. Since it was the weekend, Tomi was surprised to see her teacher in the camp.

"The classroom is such a mess. It needs to be cleaned up. Saturday seems like a good day for it," said Mrs. Glessner.

"I can help you," Tomi said.

"I would be grateful for that," her teacher replied. The two walked together to the school building and went into the classroom. "Let's take down the books and dust the shelves first. Then we can put the books back in order. I never seem to find the book I'm looking for," Mrs. Glessner said. She stood on a chair and handed down the books to Tomi. Then she found a rag and wiped the dust from the shelves. "I don't know why I do this. The dust just keeps coming back."

When the shelves were clean, Mrs. Glessner stood on the chair again, and Tomi handed her the books. Mrs. Glessner stopped and studied one of them. "So that's where this book was hiding. It's about citizenship. I promised to loan it to my friend who teaches at the Ellis school. I think you understand what citizenship is, Tomi. It's about being loyal and working for your country, like your brother's doing by serving in the army." Mrs. Glessner paused. "And you. I know you have had a difficult time here, but you're a good citizen."

"I was when I lived in California. I was a Girl Scout. We flew the flag, and I said the Pledge of Allegiance every day. But I don't know how to be one here. I live in a camp. There's nothing I can do."

Mrs. Glessner got down from the chair and set the book on the desk. "Of course there is, and you're doing it. You're working for the war effort, collecting newspapers and scrap iron. You sold raffle tickets to raise money for the 442nd. You're loyal and patriotic, too." She set the book on her desk and dusted off her hands. "The children in my friend's class are writing essays on why they're Americans. All the ninth graders in Colorado have been asked to write them. There's a contest to pick the best one, with a one-hundred dollar prize for the best essay. The winner goes to Denver to receive it from the governor."

Tomi thought about it. Then she asked, "If I'm so loyal and patriotic, why can't I write an essay? Why can't all the kids in my class write them?"

Mrs. Glessner put the dust rag down. "Why indeed? Why didn't I think of that? Of course you must write an essay, and so should everyone in your class. After all, you're ninth-grade Colorado school children." She laughed. "Even if you don't want to be."

"What are we supposed to write about?" Tomi asked.

"Whatever you like. The subject is 'Why I Am an American,' but that could include almost anything. Think it over. I'm sure you'll come up with something. You have a week to turn it in." She picked up the citizenship book and looked at it. "I'll give this to my friend. Your class won't need it. With the paper and scrap metal drives, the

Fourth of July celebration and the raffle ticket sales, you already know what citizenship is all about."

Tomi thought about the essay on the way back to her apartment, and all that evening. She was an American because she'd been born in America. But she knew there was more to it. Being an American wasn't just an accident. You *chose* to be a good American. Maybe she would write about that.

1945 | CHAPTER TWENTY-THREE

WHY POP CAME *to* AMERICA

ON MONDAY, Mrs. Glessner told the class about the essay contest. "This is not an assignment. You can skip it if you want to. But being an American is something I want you to think about," Mrs. Glessner continued. "What does it mean?"

"Being able to listen to a radio and not being cooped up in a relocation camp," one boy blurted out.

Mrs. Glessner considered what he said. Then she asked, "Does that mean that none of you are Americans?"

"No," several students answered.

"Then you can be an American and still be an internee?" she asked.

"I think it means you can be one even if you aren't treated very well," Ruth said.

Tomi grinned at her. Ruth was smart—smart enough to write a prize-winning essay. "Even if you don't agree with what your country does, it's still your country," Tomi added.

"I'm an American because my brother's in the army," a boy said.

"I'm an American because I salute the flag and say the Pledge of Allegiance every morning," a girl added.

"I like to play baseball. Does that make me an American?" another boy asked.

His friend leaned over and poked him in the ribs. "It makes you a crummy second baseman."

★

That evening, Tomi asked Pop, "Why did you come to America?"

Pop frowned at her. "Why do you ask such a question?"

Tomi shrugged. "I just wondered. If you're so unhappy living in America, why did you come here in the first place?"

When Pop didn't answer, Mom looked up from her sewing and said, "Tell her, Sam."

Pop thought that over, and finally he nodded. "All right. You know I wasn't always unhappy with this country, Tomi. I came here because I thought I would have opportunities I didn't have in Japan. There, my father was a poor man, and so was my *jiji*, my grandfather. They worked all day on a farm for a big landowner. They never had a chance to have their own farm. If I stayed, I would always be a poor man, too. I didn't want to work for someone else all day and bow to him and thank him for the little bit he paid me. I wanted something better."

"He worked very hard," Mom said. "Your *baba* told me he was the hardest-working boy in the family. And he learned English before he came here."

"But I did not speak it as well as your mother did. She studied it with a tutor. Your mother was born into a wealthy family. I was lucky to marry her."

Tomi knew the story. Mom's older sisters had married rich men. Then Tomi's grandfather lost his money gambling, and he couldn't find a husband for Mom. He decided then that Mom should marry a well-to-do American. Mom smiled at Pop. "My mother and father thought all Americans were rich. So that is why I became a picture bride. Your father looked at all the pictures of girls who wanted to marry a Japanese man in America and picked me."

"And you found out I wasn't rich," Pop said. "All I had was a silver dollar."

"I am rich in family," she told him. "I don't want anything else."

"I was very lucky when I chose your mother's picture. I did not know she could speak English. It was a nice surprise. She taught me much." Pop smiled at Mom. He didn't do that often anymore.

"I was very happy he picked me. I thought he was so handsome he could have married a movie star." She smiled back at Pop. "I still think he is handsome."

Pop patted Mom's hand. "I made a good choice. You are a good wife, even though you don't stay home anymore."

"I am an American wife," Mom said. "My husband doesn't tell me what to do."

Tomi grinned at her parents. They hadn't joked with each other much lately. She was glad she had questioned them about coming to America. She asked what it was like when Pop first arrived.

"Very confusing," Pop replied. "In the beginning, I thought I would get a job in the city. No more farming for me. No getting my hands dirty. But I didn't like so many people crowded together. I didn't like the tall buildings either. I went to work for Mr. Lawrence. He is a good man. He taught me how to farm in California." Pop frowned. "That is, he *was* a good man. I think he has forgotten about me now."

Mom shook her head. "No, no. He doesn't know where you are. That's all. We will go back when the war is over."

"Bah!" Pop said.

"Was America what *you* expected it to be, Mom?" Tomi asked.

"It was pretty good, but maybe not as good as I had expected," Mom replied. "Your pop wrote me that he lived in a big house with a servant."

"I didn't want you to get discouraged and marry somebody else," Pop said. "That's why I wrote that."

Mom laughed. "But you were right when you said America was better than Japan."

Pop nodded. "That's what I thought then. I believed that in America, I could be anything I wanted. I didn't have to be a farmer unless I chose to be. I knew if I worked hard, I could make a good living, and I was right. After all, we had a house with running water and electricity and three bedrooms. In Japan, we would have lived in one room with maybe an oil lamp, and your mother would have had to carry water from a well. Women did the hard work there."

"Women do the hard work here, too," Mom said and glanced toward Pop. "One thing I like about America is women don't have to obey the men," she said with a smile.

"I don't like that so much," Pop laughed and gave Mom a little poke, and she laughed too. "I thought America would be a better place to raise children. I chose America for you and Roy and Hiro," Pop said.

"We both chose it," Mom added. The two of them looked at each other for a long time.

Tomi couldn't remember the last time she had seen her parents enjoy themselves so much. It was almost as if they were back on the farm in California.

But then Pop frowned. "I thought it was a pretty good country, too, until the war came along. Then I learned America isn't for a Japanese man or a Japanese woman. It isn't for Japanese children who are born in America either. Even in Japan, I never saw so much hate. In America, they lock you up just because you look different. They blame you for the war because you came from Japan. The government can take everything you worked for and throw you in jail. Bah!"

"Are you sorry you came here then?" This time Mom asked the question.

Pop didn't answer, only shrugged as if he couldn't make up his mind.

"I'm not sorry," Mom said. "Even in this camp, I'm not sorry. This is a better life for me than what I had. Women can do more here than in Japan."

"In an internment camp?" Pop had turned glum again. "I came to America because I believed in it. Now I don't believe anymore."

Tomi thought that over. "Then do you believe you would be better off if you never came here?"

Pop didn't say anything for a long time. Tomi thought he wouldn't answer her. Finally he said, "Who can tell? Maybe if I had stayed in Japan, I would be fighting against America. I wouldn't like that."

"If you refused to fight in the Japanese army, maybe you would get sent to a camp worse than this one," Mom told him. "What about that?"

Pop didn't have an answer. He left then to join the old men who sat in the sun and complained. Mom sat down by the window and began stitching. Tomi pulled a chair to the table and jotted down a few notes for her essay.

"What are you writing?" Mom asked as she looked up from her sewing.

"Just homework," Tomi replied.

1945 | CHAPTER TWENTY-FOUR
ROY'S LETTER

TOMI was still thinking about what to write in her essay when Roy's weekly letter to the family arrived. He had finished basic training and had been shipped overseas to fight in Europe with the 442nd Infantry. The family was proud of him, even Pop, Tomi thought, although Pop didn't say so. There was a picture of Roy in his uniform on the table, beside a jar of paper flowers. Roy's letters were kept in a wooden box next to the vase. And in the window was a banner with a blue star to show that a member of the Itano family was fighting in the war.

Pop had been against Roy's joining the army, of course, although he admitted, "It is a good thing to be a warrior. It brings honor to the family." Once, Tomi had heard her father brag to the old men that his son would kill many enemy soldiers. "A good, brave boy," he'd said. Still, he made it clear he didn't approve of his son fighting for his country.

Roy wrote every week, addressing his letters to the entire family. Pop was the only one who was allowed to open them, however. He read them to himself. Then if he was in a good mood, he read them to the rest of the family. Sometimes, he handed a letter to Mom, who read it to Tomi and Hiro. Later, Mom read the letters over and over to herself when she was alone. More than once, Tomi came into the apartment and found Mom crying over one of Roy's letters. "I don't care if he is a good warrior," she admitted to Tomi once. "I just want him to come home."

"I know you're worried he'll get hurt," Tomi told her. She'd almost said "die" instead of "hurt," but she knew Mom didn't want to think about that possibility. Neither did Tomi.

"Of course I worry. I worry about all of my children. But I worry most about Roy. The men in the 442nd Infantry do such dangerous fighting. They have received many medals for their bravery. They also receive many Purple Heart medals because they are wounded in battle. Maybe your pop was right. Maybe Roy should have refused to enlist in the army."

"You know he would have joined no matter what Pop said."

"Maybe he wouldn't if he'd known how much his father worries about him."

"I thought you and I were the only ones who worried. Pop says if something happens to Roy, it's his own fault. He even says it would serve Roy right for disobeying his father."

Mom nodded. "Your pop is angry, all right. Still, I know that he is afraid something will happen to Roy. There are so many things that upset him these days. Pop resents that there is no work for him, while I have a job and bring in money to pay for what we need. That makes him feel useless. He believes he can no longer protect his family. After all, he couldn't keep the government from sending us to Tallgrass. He feels he is not head of our family any longer. But he worries most, I think, because he cannot keep Roy safe."

★

Tomi stared at the vase of paper flowers and thought

about what to write in her essay. Mrs. Hayashi had made the flowers for Mom the day Roy left. Tomi removed one of the flowers and studied the way the paper was folded into a shape. Then she glanced down at the wooden box where Roy's letters were kept. She returned the flower to the vase and asked, "What happened to the letter from Roy that came yesterday? It's not in the box. You never read it to us."

Mom had stopped sewing and was staring out the window. She shook her head. "I never read it either. Pop wouldn't show it to me."

Tomi frowned. "Did he open it?"

"Oh, yes. He read it and didn't say a word. He just put it into his coat pocket."

Both Mom and Tomi turned their heads to stare at Pop's coat, which was hanging on a nail on the wall. The day was warm, and Pop had left the apartment wearing his sweater.

"Where is Pop?" Tomi asked.

"He went to the canteen to drink tea with the men."

Tomi frowned. Then she asked, "Are you thinking what I'm thinking?"

Mom shook her head. "Oh, Tomi, your father would

be so angry if he found out I read Roy's letter without his permission."

"The letter wasn't just for Pop. Roy sent it to all of us. He addressed it to Mr. and Mrs. Itano, Tomi, and Hiro."

"That's true, but you know Pop believes the letters are his."

"You do other things Pop doesn't like. You work as a teacher."

"That cannot be helped." Mom put the needle into her sewing and looked out the window again. "I am afraid that Roy has been hurt and that your pop does not want me to know. He is trying to protect me."

Tomi nodded. She had been thinking that, too. She went across the room and put her hand on Mom's shoulder. Mom stared down at the sewing in her lap and gave a little laugh. "There. Look at what I've done. The stitches are so bad I will have to take them out."

"That's because you're worried. What is better, knowing or not knowing?" Tomi asked.

Mom thought that over. "I think it is not knowing. Maybe Roy was hurt only a little. I would be happy to know that. It would be better than worrying that he is in a bad way." She gave a little gasp. "What if he is dead, and

I don't know? Your father has no right to keep that from me." She put the sewing aside and stood up. "You won't tell if I open the letter, will you? I can't bear not knowing what is in it."

"Of course I won't tell. The letter is for me, too, Mom."

"I am a poor wife," Mom said.

"But you are a good mother."

Mom squeezed Tomi's shoulder. Then she went to Pop's coat and drew out the letter. She took a deep breath and opened it. "Dear family," she began. She read the letter quickly to herself, and then her eyes grew wide, and she looked up at Tomi.

"What?" Tomi asked.

"I understand now why Pop hid the letter."

Tomi came close to the paper and tried to make out the writing. "Is Roy hurt?"

"Oh, no." Mom put the letter down by her side for a moment. Then she raised it and said, "I'll read it to you." She moved her finger down the lines of writing until she found the place she wanted. Then she read,

Pop, you sent me the best present I ever got. It and Hiro's flag pin will keep me safe. I never thought you'd part with your lucky

silver dollar, because I know what it means to you. I will carry it with pride and honor until I come home and return it to you.

Mom looked up with tears in her eyes.

"Pop sent Roy his lucky dollar?" Tomi asked. She couldn't believe her father would part with it.

Mom nodded. "Pop did not want us to know. He was afraid we would think him foolish. He must be proud that Roy joined the army after all. "Mom folded the letter and put it back into Pop's pocket. She took a deep breath. "It is our secret. Now you must finish your schoolwork, Tomi."

Tomi nodded and sat back down at the table. She knew what to write in her essay. She picked up her pencil and began.

1945 | CHAPTER TWENTY-FIVE
TOMI'S ESSAY

ALMOST everyone in Tomi's class wrote essays about "Why I Am an American." Mrs. Glessner took them home that night and graded them. The next day, she handed the essays back to the students. All but Tomi's. "I will see you after class, Tomi," she said.

Tomi's face turned red, and she looked down at her desk. Mrs. Glessner didn't like her essay. Tomi had thought her idea was a good one, but now she wasn't so sure. She'd written the essay in a hurry. Perhaps it was sloppy. Mrs. Glessner wouldn't like it if she'd misspelled words or used poor grammar. Tomi hoped her teacher wouldn't visit Mom and Pop again and tell them Tomi had lost interest in her schoolwork.

Tomi fidgeted until the bell rang, ending classes for the

day.

"You want me to wait for you?" Ruth asked, as she picked up her pencil and arithmetic book.

Tomi shook her head. She'd be embarrassed if Ruth heard Mrs. Glessner bawl her out.

After the other students left, Tomi went to the front of the room and stood beside Mrs. Glessner's desk.

"Sit down," the teacher said.

Tomi swallowed. Sitting down meant a long conversation. "Yes, ma'am," she said.

"I read your essay last night. In fact, I read it four times," Mrs. Glessner began.

"I'm sorry if ..." Tomi started to say, but Mrs. Glessner held up her hand.

"And I find it the finest writing you have ever done." Mrs. Glessner smiled.

"Really?" Tomi couldn't believe she had heard right.

"In fact, it is the best in the class."

Tomi's mouth dropped open. "I thought you didn't like it."

"You did? Why?"

"Well, you didn't give it back. And you asked me to stay after school."

Mrs. Glessner smiled again. "Oh, I'm sorry. I made you worry. But you see, I couldn't talk about it with you in front of the class."

Tomi didn't understand.

"I want you to recopy it. You crossed out some words, and one word is misspelled. I want it to be perfect."

"Why?"

"Because I'm going to enter it into the Colorado essay contest. It will be Tallgrass's entry. I didn't want the class to know because, well, Tallgrass wasn't exactly invited to participate in the contest. I think it was an oversight, but who knows?" Mrs. Glessner said.

Tomi stared at her teacher, and her eyes grew big. *Her* essay was going to be in the contest! But how could that be if Tallgrass students hadn't been invited to submit entries?

Mrs. Glessner looked uneasy. "I hope you will understand what I am going to say," she said and waited until Tomi nodded before she continued. "I've asked one of the teachers at the Ellis school to send it in with the Ellis entries."

Tomi thought for a minute. "Would the judges throw it out if they knew it came from a Japanese girl at Tallgrass?"

"I don't know that for sure, but I wouldn't want to take

a chance. It's not right to have to mislead them, of course. But it wouldn't be fair if you were eliminated because you are Japanese either. This way, your essay will have an equal chance with all the others. Your work will be judged on its merits, not on the race of the person who wrote it."

"But what about my name? The judges will know I'm Japanese if they see my name."

"Tomi Itano. You know, it sounds Italian to me," said Mrs. Glessner.

★

Of course, Tomi didn't expect to win. But she was thrilled that her essay was good enough to be entered in the contest. She carefully copied it, then gave it to Mrs. Glessner. When the two of them agreed it was perfect, Tomi folded up the original and put it inside her book.

Ruth was playing outside when Tomi left the classroom. Tomi was surprised to see her. After all, she had stayed in the classroom for a long time. "What did Mrs. Glessner want?" Ruth asked.

Tomi shrugged. "I had a misspelled word in my paper."

"It must have been an awfully long word."

"Oh, we got to talking." Tomi didn't tell Ruth about her essay. Ruth might think she was showing off. Besides, her entry was a secret.

Hiro came up to her then. "Wilson and I are going to play baseball. Want to watch us?"

"Sure," Tomi said, glad to change the subject.

"Ruth said you had to stay after school," he said. "Were you bad?"

Tomi laughed and poked her brother in the arm. "Not as bad as you are as a baseball player."

"Hey, I hit a double last time I was at bat." Hiro played baseball every chance he could.

"Dumb luck," Wilson teased him.

Tomi thought again how fortunate the younger kids were that they had adjusted to the camp. She wondered if Hiro had forgotten about the farm where they had lived. Maybe that would be a good thing.

But he hadn't forgotten. "When we go home to California, everybody's going to be surprised at how good I am. I'll be the first one picked when we choose up teams."

"You're kidding yourself. Those guys have gotten better, too. They have good baseballs and bats, better ones than we do. And they have those fancy ball fields with grass. No dirt fields like Tallgrass," Wilson said.

"That just means we're tougher."

"Come on, tough guys. You're not playing at all unless you get to the ball field," Tomi told the two boys.

As they walked to the field, Hiro said, "I'm glad you like to watch me play baseball, Tomi. Pop never comes to see me play. Everybody else's dad does. Even Helen comes to see Wilson."

"Maybe he doesn't like baseball," Tomi said.

"Sure he does. He went to all of Roy's games in California. And remember how he used to play catch with me? Maybe he doesn't like me," Hiro said quietly.

Tomi put her arm around Hiro. "Of course he likes you, Hiro. Pop loves his family. He's just unhappy with America."

"What can we do?"

Tomi sighed. "I don't know. Mom doesn't either. Maybe when the war is over, Pop will turn into the old Pop."

"I hope so," Hiro said. "I miss him."

★

"Tomi had to stay after school," Hiro announced when they went inside the apartment after the baseball game.

Both Mom and Pop looked up from what they were doing. Pop frowned. "What did you do?" he asked.

"We don't know that she did anything," Mom said. "Maybe she just helped clean the blackboards."

"We don't have blackboards," Tomi said. She shrugged. "It wasn't anything."

"Not anything?" Pop said. "You have to stay after school, and it's not anything?"

"You haven't lost interest again, have you?" Mom asked.

"Mrs. Glessner just wanted to talk to me about my essay," Tomi explained.

Mom put down her sewing. She was using scraps of the blue cotton that Mrs. Hayashi had given her to make a pillow. "Did she like it?"

Tomi shrugged. "I guess. She made me recopy it." She looked down at the floor. "I had a misspelling, and some of the words were crossed out. She said I was sloppy."

"Serves you right," Pop said.

Mom fitted two tiny pieces of blue together and pinned them. "I would like to read it, Tomi. Wouldn't you,

Sam? Tomi says it's called 'Why I'm an American.' "

"No." Pop picked up the camp newspaper. "Tomi's a Japanese American. That's not any kind of American at all." He began reading again.

"Well, I still want to read it," Mom said, putting aside her sewing.

"You can't," Tomi said. "It's at school."

Later, Tomi remembered she had put the original copy of her essay into her book, but she didn't say anything about that. She didn't want Mom to read it. What if Mom said Tomi had no business writing what she did?

1945 | CHAPTER TWENTY-SIX
THE WINNER

IN APRIL, the war in Europe was over! Victory in Europe, or VE Day, the end of that war was called. Tomi heard the whistle go off at the sugar beet factory in Ellis. Then there were the sounds of firecrackers and car horns. In a few minutes, the school principal rushed into the classroom to announce that Germany had surrendered. The children cheered, and Mrs. Glessner asked them to stand and say the Pledge of Allegiance. Then they sang "The Star-Spangled Banner."

Mrs. Glessner dismissed the class, and the children ran outside. There weren't many schoolchildren left at Tallgrass. Most of the men at the camp had taken jobs in Denver and moved away. Some had left Colorado for work in other states. Pop refused to get a job, which was why the Itanos had remained in the camp. Fortunately for Tomi, Mr. Hayashi worked in the camp office, so Ruth had stayed at Tallgrass, too.

Although Helen had hated the camp when she arrived, she chose to stay on after she graduated from high school. She said Mrs. Hayashi was like a grandmother to Carl, and she didn't want to take him away from her. Besides, if Helen found employment outside the camp, who would look after Carl and Wilson? But Tomi thought Helen was really waiting for Roy to come back. And he would come back. The war was over, and Roy was safe!

Now the children stood near the school, shouting, "The war's over!" and "We won!" Those who had bikes tied red, white, or blue scarves to the handlebars. Hiro rushed around yelling, "Whatcha know, Joe? Do you know it's VE Day?" Tomi and Ruth ran home to the Itanos' apartment, where they found Mom making tea. Mr. and Mrs. Hayashi and Carl were there.

"Did you hear?" Tomi yelled as she came through the door. "The war is over."

"Only in Europe. There's still a war in Japan." Pop said.

"But it will be over there soon," Mom told him. Mr. and Mrs. Hayashi brought special tea to celebrate. It is very good tea. It came with them from San Francisco."

"I saved it for a celebration," Mrs. Hayashi said. "And what better celebration than that the war is over and we won!"

"Why do we care?" Pop asked. "America still thinks we are the enemy."

"You're a spoilsport, Sam. I, for one, am a true blue American," Mr. Hayashi told him.

"You are just in time," Mom said to Tomi. She had heated water on the stove. Now she poured it into the china pot and set out her best tea cups. She let the tea steep. Then Mom poured it into the fragile cups and handed them around.

"To American victory," Mr. Hayashi toasted. He raised his cup. Ruth and Tomi, along with their mothers and Carl, raised their cups, too, and at last, so did Pop.

"Are they going to close the camp now?" Mrs. Hayashi asked.

"Not yet," Pop told her. "America hasn't beaten the Japanese. We have to stay here."

"Nobody has to stay here. There are jobs all over America for us," Mr. Hayashi said. "You're just stubborn, Sam."

"No jobs in California," Pop told him. "They don't want us there."

"There will be jobs soon enough."

"Not for me," Pop said.

"No more unhappy words," Mom told him.

Pop was quiet then, as the others talked about VE Day. Mom fixed more tea. Then the Hayashis went home, and Pop left to sit in the sun with the old men. Tomi fetched a bucket of water, which Mom heated on the stove, and the two washed the teapot and cups.

"I thought Pop would be excited about Victory in Europe," Tomi said, as she picked up Mom's delicate cup.

"Sometimes I think he is tired of complaining, but he doesn't know how to stop. I think he would like to be the old Pop again, but he doesn't know how."

Mom started to say more, but Ruth came back into the apartment and asked Tomi to go into Ellis with her. "Father gave me money for ice cream," she said. So the two walked down the dirt road to Ellis where people were waving flags and blowing toy horns. A band played. A girl handed Tomi a noisemaker and yelled, "We won! We won!" At the drug store, a man was giving away ice cream to everyone. "Here, girls, have some ice cream. It's VE Day!"

he cried, handing cones to Ruth and Tomi. "Tell everybody at Tallgrass to come in for free ice cream." Nobody called Ruth and Tomi Japs.

"Maybe Pop's the only one who remembers we're still fighting Japan," Tomi said. "I wish he'd come here to Ellis and see how people are treating us."

"Will he?" Ruth asked.

"I don't think so."

★

The following day, the children were still too excited to pay attention in class. They talked about the German surrender and how they could all go home now that the war was over.

"But we're still at war with Japan," Ruth said in a loud voice.

"What does that mean, Mrs. Glessner?" a boy asked.

"It means that Japan no longer has any allies—friends to help them fight. The American army is beating the Japanese army. So the end of the war in Europe means the war with Japan will be over soon. Then Tallgrass will be closed. You'll be allowed to go wherever you want to, even

California."

"Does that mean they'll let us be Americans?" Ruth asked.

Mrs. Glessner smiled. "You already are. You've always been Americans. You are Americans because your parents chose America for you."

Tomi turned red and looked down. Those were words from her essay. She hoped Mrs. Glessner wouldn't read it to the class. The contest had been over for a long time, and if she'd won, she'd have heard about it by now. If Mrs. Glessner read the essay, the others would know it was the Tallgrass entry in the contest and that it had lost. Tomi would feel she'd let everyone down.

"I have something to tell you, something that will make you proud," Mrs. Glessner said. "I was going to announce it yesterday, but we were all too busy celebrating Victory in Europe." She paused, then continued. "Most of you wrote essays about 'Why I Am an American.' They were very good, but the best of them was Tomi Itano's. That was why I entered it in the state contest."

Mrs. Glessner paused and smiled at Tomi, while Tomi slunk lower in her seat. This was awful. Now the whole class would know she was a loser.

"The state judges thought it was the best, too, because they awarded it *first prize!*"

Tomi stared at Mrs. Glessner in surprise. "I won?" she mouthed. She sat up straight.

"Yes, you won," Mrs. Glessner said.

"My essay won?" Tomi couldn't believe it.

Mrs. Glessner nodded.

"First place?"

"First place. Your essay was the best one in the whole state."

"But I'm Japanese," Tomi said.

"What does that have to do with being an American?" her teacher asked.

Tomi was too stunned to say anything more, but Ruth wasn't. "Hooray for Tomi!" Ruth yelled, and the students clapped.

"Read your essay," a boy said.

"Yeah, Tomi, read it," another student added.

Tomi blushed. She didn't want to stand up in front of the class and read her words. "I don't have it. Mrs. Glessner sent it in," she said.

"I sent in the copy you rewrote. What about the original? Don't you have it?" the teacher asked.

"Oh, I guess I still do," Tomi replied.

"You don't have to read it in class," Mrs. Glessner said, and Tomi breathed a sigh of relief. "Instead, you can read it at the VE celebration in the camp this afternoon."

Tomi slunk back in her chair. That was terrible. She'd have to stand up before the whole camp. But that wasn't what frightened her most. She'd have to read it in front of Pop.

1945 | CHAPTER TWENTY-SEVEN
WHY I AM *an* AMERICAN

"WE'RE wearing our best clothes to the VE Day celebration," Mom said when Tomi went back to the apartment. Mom had put on a white kimono with big pink flowers on it. "Hurry, Tomi. We don't want to be late."

"Is Pop going?" Tomi asked. Pop didn't attend many camp events, and Tomi hoped he would stay home.

"Of course, he is. This is a big day."

Tomi glanced at her father, who was wearing his suit and a tie. He stood looking out the window, holding his hat. "I don't know why I should go. I'd rather stay here," he said.

"It's not a big deal," Tomi said, hoping she could talk her father out of it.

"It's a very big deal," Mom told her. "We won the war

in Europe."

Hiro burst into the room then and yelled, "Tomi won some essay contest about being an American. She beat everybody in the state! The whole school's talking about it."

Mom turned to Tomi in surprise. "Oh, that's wonderful! Why didn't you tell us?"

Tomi shrugged.

"She's going to read it at the celebration," Hiro continued. Tomi sent him a fierce look to shut him up, but he only grinned at her.

"Then we will be very happy," Mom told her. "Now, Sam, that is a good reason to go to the celebration. You would shame your daughter if you stayed home. I won't let you."

"Won't let me? You sound like an American woman telling her husband what to do."

"I am an American woman," Mom told him.

"Bah," Pop said.

Tomi sat down on her bed, thinking she might say she had a stomach ache and had to stay in the apartment, but she knew Mom wouldn't let her get away with that.

"Hurry up. Put on your red dress," Mom said, removing

the dress from a nail on the wall. Tomi went behind the curtain that divided the room and changed into the dress as slowly as she could. "It's too small. I look awful. Everybody will laugh at me," she said. Indeed, the dress came above her knees, and it pulled across her waist. "I've had this since we lived in California."

"Then we will buy you a new one when we go back there," Mom said. "Other girls are wearing tight dresses, too. Come along."

Tomi dragged her feet as the four of them walked to the big open space in camp where meetings were held. Mom took Tomi's arm to pull her along and whispered, "Don't be nervous. Remember what a hard time I had standing in front of the quilt class the first time? Now I don't mind it at all."

But Tomi wasn't worried about getting up in front of people. She was worried about what Pop would say when he heard her essay. She glanced up at one of the towers and realized there were no longer any guards. Was that because of VE Day or had they disappeared a long time ago? She was so used to the towers that she hadn't noticed.

As soon as they reached the crowd, Tomi went off in search of Ruth. Maybe it would start raining or the stage would cave in before it was her turn to speak. Then she wouldn't have to read her essay. The essay had been a bad idea, a terrible idea. Pop would be furious.

The victory ceremony started only minutes after the Itanos arrived, and Tomi knew nothing could stop her now from having to read the essay. There were prayers and speeches. A band played "God Bless America" and "America the Beautiful" and then the national anthem, as people sang. The ceremony lasted a long time, and Tomi hoped she'd been forgotten. But then a man announced, "We have a special surprise. Just this week, one of our students, Tomi Itano, won a state contest with her essay, 'Why I Am an American.' Now Tomi's going to read it to us."

People clapped as Tomi slowly made her way to the stage. Her hands were sweaty, and her knees shook. As she climbed the steps, she looked around for Mom and Pop. At first she couldn't find them, but then she saw them right in the front! Now there was no way Pop wouldn't hear her words. Tomi took a deep breath. There was nothing she could do about it. *Shikata ga nai*, she thought; it can't be helped. So she might as well get it over with. She unfolded the essay she had kept in her book and began in a small voice, " 'Why I Am an American' ..."

"Louder," someone called.

Tomi raised her voice and repeated, " 'Why I Am an American,' by Tomi Itano."

Her hand shook as she raised the paper. Then, slowly, she began to read. "The day my father arrived on America's shore, he found a silver dollar lying in the street." Tomi looked down at Pop feeling even more nervous.

"He kept that silver dollar. There were times during his first days in this country that he could have spent it to buy food or a place to sleep. But he wouldn't part with it, because it was his lucky dollar. He told me that every time he looked at it, he remembered the luckiest day of his life, the day he came to America."

Tomi stopped and glanced again at Pop. He had removed his hat and was turning it around and around in his hands.

Tomi gulped and went on. "The first sound I remember hearing when I was a little girl was my father jingling that coin against pennies and nickels in his pocket. Not long ago, however, I stopped hearing it. That's because my father no longer has the silver dollar. He sent it to my brother Roy, who is serving in the U.S. Army in Europe. The dollar was such powerful good luck that he gave it to

Roy to keep him safe. And it has."

Tomi looked at Pop. To her surprise, Pop was standing up straight, his head held high. Mom reached over and took his hand.

Swallowing again, Tomi continued her essay. "In the old country, Pop knew he couldn't go far. By law, everything in the family was inherited by the first son. Pop was the third son. But in America, everyone had an equal chance. If he worked hard, he could have his own home, with running water and a bedroom for each of his children. He could build his own business. His children would be free to choose their future, too. He came to America not just for himself but for his children.

"Pop's business was a strawberry farm, and one day, he pointed to the red berries, white clouds, and blue sky. He told me those were the colors of the American flag, the flag we raised in our front yard every morning. It was the flag of *his* country—and mine.

"My father is an American because he chose to be one." Tomi looked up at the crowd and concluded, "And I am an American because he chose America for me."

As Tomi finished, people clapped. A few cheered and whistled. Pop clapped the loudest. Then, before Tomi could leave the platform, he jumped up beside her. He bowed to the audience, then held up his hand, and people grew quiet. "I am Tomi Itano's father," he announced. "And I am the proudest man at Tallgrass." Then he took Tomi's hand, and the two walked off the stage.

Tomi was so shocked that at first, she couldn't speak. Then she said, "I thought you wouldn't like my essay, Pop. I thought you'd be mad that Mom and I found out about your silver dollar."

"Oh, I knew you would. I know Mom reads all of Roy's letters. American women do that, and she's an American woman."

"And you're an American man," Tomi said.

Pop looked at Tomi a long time. "I had almost forgotten that," Pop said softly. And then he added, "You reminded me, Tomi. Thank you."

1945 | CHAPTER TWENTY-EIGHT
TOMI MEETS *the* GOVERNOR

AT THE end of the VE Day celebration, Mrs. Glessner came up to Mom and Pop and Tomi. "I have your tickets. "You take the train first thing Monday morning."

Pop looked confused. "What train?"

Mrs. Glessner frowned. "Didn't Tomi tell you? The governor himself is presenting Tomi with her award. The whole family, even Hiro, has been invited to the ceremony."

"We're going to Denver, on the train?" Pop asked.

"Yes, the judges are paying for the train tickets," Mrs. Glessner said.

Mom smoothed her kimono and asked, "Does the governor know we're Japanese?"

Mrs. Glessner laughed. "He will soon enough. But don't worry. Governor Carr has a Japanese housekeeper."

"Do the judges know?" Tomi asked.

"I didn't tell them," Mrs. Glessner said. "But then, nobody asked. The contest was open to all American ninth-graders in Colorado, and Tomi's an American."

Pop grinned. "So am I."

★

Two women stood on the platform at Union Station, the train depot in Denver, looking around. One of them held a sign that said: "Tomi Itano." When Tomi approached them, they ignored her.

"Excuse me," Tomi said.

One of the women glanced at Tomi, then looked past her to watch the people getting off the train. "Yes," she said.

"I'm Tomi Itano."

At first, the woman didn't seem to hear her. She craned her neck to look down the track. Then she turned back and stared at Tomi. "What?" she said.

"I'm Tomi Itano."

"We're looking for a boy who won an essay contest," the second woman said. She had stopped watching the passengers and was staring at Tomi.

"I'm Tomi Itano. I'm a girl, not a boy. I won the contest. I go to school at Tallgrass in Ellis."

The woman frowned. "You wrote an essay on 'Why I Am an American'"?

Oh, no, Tomi thought, as she nodded. What if the women refused to let her win? What if they told her to get back on the train to Ellis?

The two women looked at each other. "We chose an essay by a Japanese girl from an internment camp?" one of them said.

The other nodded. "Can you beat that!"

"Well, good for us." She held out her hand. "Tomi Itano, I'm glad to meet you. I'm Mrs. Bennett, and this is Mrs. Knowles."

Tomi grinned. Then she introduced Mom and Pop and Hiro, and Pop shook the two women's hands.

"So you're the man with the silver dollar?" Mrs. Knowles said.

"I'm the *American* with the silver dollar," Pop told her.

"Yes, you are. You are a surprise," Mrs. Bennett said.

"Didn't you know Tomi was a Japanese girl?" Hiro asked.

"I thought maybe she was an Italian boy," Mrs. Bennett replied. "But it doesn't matter what you are, does it? Come along. The governor is waiting for us." The two women led them to a big black car and told the driver to take them to the state capitol.

Tomi had never been to Denver before, and she stared at the capitol building with its gold dome. But not for long, because the women hurried them up the steps, and they walked down a long marble hallway to the governor's office.

"This is Tomi Itano, the girl who won the state essay contest," Mrs. Bennett told the receptionist.

At that, a man with a big camera came up to them and said, "I'm from the *Denver Post*. What a great story this will make. We'll put it on the front page."

The receptionist went into an office, then came back and motioned for everyone to enter. A man behind a desk stood up and said, "So you're the little girl who wrote about her father's silver dollar. What a nice surprise this is. I'm Governor Carr." He held out his hand. Then he shook hands with Mom and Pop and even Hiro. He turned to the photographer. "Bill, you better get a picture of this. It's a mighty good story. People ought to know about the kind of *Americans* we put into those relocation camps. Maybe one day we'll ask them to forgive us for what we did to them."

The governor came around his desk to stand beside Tomi and her family. He presented Tomi with a certificate and a check for a hundred dollars. The photographer lifted his camera, and a flashbulb went off.

"By the way," the governor asked when they were finished. "Did your son Roy come through the war okay?"

"You bet," Pop grinned. "He'll be coming home any day now."

The receptionist came into the room then and said, "Sir, your next appointment is waiting."

"Well, let him wait," Governor Carr said. Then he turned to Pop. "My housekeeper is Japanese. She was at the internment camp in Wyoming. I don't know what I'd do without her. What say you come home with me for lunch? She sure would like to meet all of you."

Pop grinned. "Ah, she is an American, too."

"You bet," the governor said. "By the way, Mr. Itano, I have something for you to jingle until Roy comes home." He reached into his pocket, then handed Pop a silver dollar.

★

Two weeks later, Pop received a letter. "It's from Mr. Lawrence," he announced. "I'll read it to you so you don't have to sneak a look at it when I'm out." Pop grinned at Mom. He chuckled a little as he took his time opening the envelope, but at last, he removed a note and began to read.

"Out loud," Mom said.

Pop laughed. "It starts 'Dear Sam.'"

Mom waved her hand. "I know that."

"He says,

We didn't know where you were until we saw an article in the newspaper here in California about Tomi receiving an award. The story must have been published in papers all across the country. You sure looked proud in the picture.

We want you to know that your house and farm are waiting for you whenever you want to come back. We rented it to a young couple, but we told them they could stay only until you returned. They are nice people, but they can't grow strawberries like you do, Sam. Nobody can.

It won't always be easy for you here, because there are still people in California who do not like the Japanese. But I think you can deal with them. You've been through a lot, and it hasn't broken your spirit.

Let me know when you will arrive. I'll meet your train. I'll bring Martha with me. She can hardly wait to see Tomi again. She told me to send you this photograph with the picture of Tomi's doll in it. There's a note from Martha, too."

Pop fished in the envelope and took out a picture of Martha, who had been Tomi's best friend in California.

Tomi studied the photograph. There was Martha holding Janice, the Japanese doll Tomi's grandparents had sent her. Janice had been Tomi's favorite possession, and she'd asked Martha to take care of the doll for her. She smiled, remembering how carefully she had played with Janice, because the doll was fragile. Then she frowned. Janice had once worn a beautiful kimono. Now she was dressed in a brown suit. Why had Martha changed the doll's clothes? Had Martha been ashamed that Janice was Japanese? Had the other girls teased Martha because she had a Japanese doll?

"See what she wrote," Pop said, handing Tomi the note.

Tomi sighed and opened the folded paper. Then she read out loud.

Hi, Tomi.

I kept Janice safe on a shelf in my room. Can you see that I made new clothes for her? I'm not very good at sewing, so you probably can't tell she's wearing an army uniform.

Tomi read the rest to herself, then she looked up with a smile. "Listen to this," she told Mom and Pop. And then she read Martha's last sentence.

I thought Janice should wear the uniform because she's a one-hundred-percent American, just like the rest of the Itanos.

AUTHOR'S NOTE

In February 1942, just two months after America went to war with Japan, President Franklin Roosevelt signed executive order 9066. It allowed the government to force more than 100,000 Japanese men, women, and children living on the West Coast to leave their homes and relocate to camps in the interior of the United States. Many of these people had been born in America and were U.S. citizens. Some couldn't speak Japanese and had never even been outside the U.S. Nonetheless, the government feared they would aid the enemy in Japan and should be moved away from the Pacific Ocean. Although the U.S. was also at war with Germany and Italy, it did not round up Germans and Italians and send them inland.

The camps were not prisons. They were *relocation*

camps. The idea was the Japanese would live there only until they found employment. They were expected to work for the war effort or to replace men who had been drafted into the U.S. Army. Many did indeed find jobs and leave. Some, however, spent the duration of the war in the camps.

The government built ten relocation camps, all of them located in remote, inhospitable areas from California to Arkansas. One of those camps was Amache, near Granada in southeast Colorado. Some 10,000 Japanese spent part or all of the war at Amache.

I renamed Amache Tallgrass, and *Red Berries, White Clouds, Blue Sky* is the second novel I've set in that camp. The first, an adult novel titled *Tallgrass*, is about a farm family living adjacent to the camp, and it's told from the standpoint of a young Caucasian girl. *Red Berries, White Clouds, Blue Sky* is from the opposite viewpoint. It is a fictional story of twelve-year-old Tomi Itano, a Japanese girl from California. It tells of one girl's struggle to understand discrimination and help her family cope with the effects of the uprooting of their lives.

Incidentally, not one single Japanese person in America was ever found guilty of World War II espionage. And the 442nd Infantry, made up of Japanese soldiers, was the most decorated army unit in U.S. history.

I learned about the relocation camps in the early 1960s, about fifteen years after Amache was closed. I'd gone pheasant hunting in southeastern Colorado with a rancher friend, who took me to see the Amache site. All that was left were dirt roads and cement slabs where buildings once stood. Since I'd never heard of World War II relocation camps, I went to the library to find out about them. In researching Amache, I discovered that after the camp was abandoned, some of its barracks were sold to the University of Denver for use as classrooms. My journalism classes at DU in the 1950s were held in one of them.

In my early years as a reporter for *Business Week* magazine in Denver, I met a number of Japanese journalists who had been interned at Amache and at Heart Mountain in Wyoming, another relocation camp. They had come to Denver at the war's end. Among them was Carl Iwasaki, a freelance photographer for *Time*, *Life*, *Sports Illustrated*, and *Business Week*. Carl, a lifelong friend, is the subject of an acclaimed book, *Japanese American Resettlement through the Lens: Hikaru Carl Iwasaki and the WRA's Photographic Section, 1943–1945*. I've fictionalized one of his poignant stories in *Red Berries, White Clouds, Blue Sky*.

My interest in Amache was rekindled many years after I visited the site when I read Robert Harvey's outstanding book *Amache: The Story of Japanese Internment in Colorado During World War II*. That book inspired me to write *Tallgrass* and eventually *Red Berries, White Clouds, Blue Sky*.

ACKNOWLEDGMENTS

When I wrote *Tallgrass*, my adult novel, published in 2007, I considered telling the story from the standpoint of a Japanese girl interned in the camp. I decided that would be presumptuous, however, since I'm not Japanese. But Amy Lennex, my editor at Sleeping Bear Press, persuaded me to tackle it. Thanks, Amy, and thanks for the questions and suggestions that made this a better book. And thanks, Danielle Egan-Miller and Joanna MacKenzie, for encouraging me to write a second children's book. Nobody ever had better agents.

I am indebted to Robert Harvey, whose *Amache: The Story of Japanese Internment in Colorado During World War II* rekindled my interest in relocation camps. Kayoko Morton was kind enough to critique the manuscript and tell me where I had gone wrong with Japanese culture. Among other things, she taught me that Japanese women use wet, crumpled newspaper when sweeping floors and that they drink tea from cups, not bowls.

My thanks to Carl Iwasaki, whose book *Japanese American Resettlement through the Lens: Hikaru Carl Iwasaki and the WRA's Photographic Section, 1943–1945* chronicles the lives of Japanese who left the camps. During my fifty-plus-year friendship with Carl, I've learned much from him. And I am especially grateful to Forrest Athearn for insisting that Roy should come through the war safely.

Thanks to my family—Bob, Dana, Kendal, Lloyd, and Forrest—for understanding this second childhood.